Praise for *Symbiosis*

With style and élan, Milagros Lasarte explores middle-class social mores in this delicious – and deliciously wicked – debut novella. It is not without compassion, however. This, coupled with Lasarte's defining leftfield sensibility, renders the familiar yet strange organism of LV irresistible. Enormously satisfying ... this is a tale that will blossom in the imagination long after it is set down.

Jane McKie
author of *Carnation Lily Lily Rose*

The cultural microcosm of the typical neighborhood is the perfect setting for Symbiosis, with a deliciously uncomfortable gander into the human tendency to create an "Us v. Them" mentality in everyday life. Debut author Milagros Lasarte nails this engrossing contemplation of societal norms with a thought-provoking twist at the end that I'm still thinking about days later. An entertaining must read from an author who is sure to be your new favorite.

Leanne Kale Sparks
award-winning author of the *Kendall Beck* series

Milagros Lasarte's fascinating debut novel is an insightful – and incisive – study on the synergies between individuals and groups, between social stasis and change. Partly allegory, partly suburban gothic, this novel examines the forces that bring together humans and their environment, creating an uneasy and tense atmosphere, where trivial or minor daily gestures or decisions threaten to unleash chaos at every turn. This is done with an assured, light-handed, and slightly ironic touch that make the novel an absolute pleasure to read.

Ioulia Kolovou
author of *The Stone Maidens*

Symbiosis

MILAGROS LASARTE

Content

The living together of unlike organisms.

Heinrich Anton de Bary

THE SYSTEM

In her alienness, she had commanded respect.

We learned to fear, not her differences, but rather the way she manipulated what little common ground we had so as to pull us into her Fever. We were fooled by those moments of vulnerability, by the awkward candour of her responses. They were elements of her personality that we held onto, for comfort.

Our System, however, was convinced her essence would damage us. It had found a strange component within her, something unlike anything it had seen before and which she herself didn't seem to acknowledge. It sent us a first signal of warning – but because of this mysterious component, the signal remained incomplete, and she managed to get through our defences.

We didn't think much of it then, and we welcomed her in.

She was looking for a new home to settle into and offered to take care of one of our defective cells. The re-polished structure of the cell still stands today, firm and functional, proving in its survival that the main issue had never been in her intentions but in the inherent impossibility of her existing as a member of our community.

Our efforts to understand each other were in vain. Whenever we took a step forward, our defences reminded us to push her away. She was just as hesitant. We kept delaying the inevitable.

For only an adaptive immune system can lead to immunological memory – but at what cost? And when reconstructing the chain of events, what is to be remembered?

PART ONE

THE RISE OF THE HOVEL

If we look deep inside our drawers, we may still find the card, small and plain, with black ink letters: our invitation to Monica's housewarming. The card had been left in our mailboxes a week after her move. By that time, some of us had already left for the summer, but those who stayed on our street made it their duty to attend the event. Any earlier plans could be cancelled. We had to examine for ourselves what transformations had been made to no. 8 – The Hovel, as we called it – and above all, understand the terms of this new ownership.

We say 'transformations,' but the changes Monica made, though improving the overall quality of the house, were unable to deconstruct its original makeup: two clean layers of grey paint covered the grime of the outer walls; the metal railings were painted over with a black veneer; and once inside we discovered that the yellow velour of the couch and the green-blue walls in the kitchen were perhaps considered modern, but still reflected the hippie energy of the previous owners. Monica would later reveal the house had spoken to her, guided her in her search for inspiration.

It didn't surprise us. No paint or trendy furniture could conceal years of negligence, or the settlement of dogs for that matter. Abandoned inside The Hovel by one of the hippies, these dogs had taken over the ground floor before slowly making their way up. Some man, whose relation to the hippies always escaped us, came to feed them regularly. He was the only human, the only living creature besides them, allowed inside the house. Until he stopped coming. As the days passed, we could hear the dogs growing restless: barking, fighting, pushing the furniture around. Then there was silence. Had they perished, their bodies decomposing on the ground floor?

After the disappearance of the dogs, the owners decided to cut all ties with The Hovel. They had never properly owned it anyway, lacking commitment, care, or any kind of constant presence. The house was then put up for sale, and the solitude suited it well. On the very edge of ruin, this new taste of freedom seemed to stabilise it.

But the house couldn't cleanse itself of the excess of turbulent energy. Residues of it must have nestled inside its porous walls, becoming part of its composition, a lingering aftertaste. Therefore, after having enjoyed its moment of peace, The Hovel was in want of someone new to roam its rooms. A few

people ventured inside, but none were deemed suit-
able guests, until Monica arrived.

To this day, it is unclear to us whether The Hovel
attracted a personality suited to its perversity, or if
said perversity eventually got to her.

1

The first one to lay eyes on the new arrival was Lise, who lived opposite The Hovel, at no. 5. She was walking back from the school, where she had just dropped off her youngest, and saw three silhouettes moving inside the house.

Her first reactionary instinct was to think, *squatters*, and slightly disturbed by this thought, she stopped to study the silhouettes with a little more objectivity. Most likely these were relatives of whoever owned The Hovel. The children of that last woman, or maybe the children of those? She squinted, stepped a bit closer, and decided these were decent people. Decent clothes, decent bearing, and the shiny black car parked at the entrance had to be theirs.

Prospective buyers. She had seen some of them before. Three actually. They didn't own a shiny car. They had walked into The Hovel with nervous expectation and a smile which suggested that, more than the house itself, it was the idea of possessing something, anything at all, which brought them here. Nervous disillusion walked them out. Upon seeing these new candidates, however, Lise felt uncharacteristically excited. She ran into her kitchen, the window there offering the greatest vantage point. Fresh conversation, maybe playmates for the children…

Wouldn't it be lovely if they all became close friends?

Her enthusiasm was based on two facts.

The first was that she saw in these candidates the opportunity to train someone new. You see, Lise thought of herself as our spiritual guide. She had assigned herself this curious title upon reaching twenty years of residence on our street – which wasn't the highest record among us, but a span of life that did encompass various significant events: her semi-rebel teenage years, experiments as a young adult and, eventually, motherhood. Lise had visited other territories in the early months of her marriage, but she couldn't fight the reassuring pull of familiarity for too long.

She claimed she was aware of all the things happening on our street, the flows and tides of our moods, and Lise strived to help the community by reinforcing the ties between us – one never knows when friendships can be utilised in the future. In the end, she had no concrete proof that her spiritual awareness worked, beyond the fact that the business of our street had, until then, never deviated from what she thought was the right path.

The second reason for her enthusiasm was that she believed she somehow was responsible for the silhouettes' visit (*a couple and their real-estate agent* was her final verdict). Only a few weeks before, Lise had told her husband, Rob, that the street was suffering from stale air. She had noticed there was a hint of grumpiness in our conversations, peaking whenever the weather was particularly bad and humid. The only rapid solution she could find was to bring new vegetation to our street – so she researched exotic plants and ordered a few seeds online. Her package never came, but on the week the delivery was due, the shiny black car parked itself outside no. 8.

When these prospective buyers eventually emerged from The Hovel, Lise grabbed her keys and rushed back outside. *What of it?* She was just checking if she had any mail. She looked so natural, walking over to her fence, opening her mailbox and turning around when the visitors reached their car – *oh, hello there, visiting the house, so very nice to meet you, so what did you think of it, forgive me, it's not my place, maybe we'll see each other again, have a good day!* So natural and smooth – at least, that is what she said to her sister, later that afternoon.

Anne didn't show the same level of fascination, but if decent people were moving in, then it meant she would finally have a nicer view when looking out of her bedroom window.

2

The news of prospective buyers travelled fast, though weeks passed before anyone saw the couple again and, filled with expectations, we assigned Anne and Lise the role of lookouts.

We thought this delay might mean they didn't have the necessary funds. The house was in a dreadful state, but this was LV, after all: there were prestigious names among our standing and long-lost residents; not everyone could afford to live on our street. Or, they might have been warned about the hippies, the dogs, and the old woman (was *she* the hippie?), the one who had died in the master bedroom. The exact timeline of events still eludes us, making it impossible to tell which of all those previous inhabitants committed the greatest ravages.

To our general surprise, however, they returned. Well, *she* did – alone. The agent was also there, but not the husband. The woman stayed inside for a whole hour, then left as quietly as she had come. Over the following month, she repeated the same routine a few more times. Was she still looking to be convinced by the house, searching for that one hidden asset that would ultimately overshadow the general decay of the walls? At some point, we wondered if the woman mightn't simply be the architect and we were wasting our social energy on the wrong individual. In any case, these comings and goings signalled that a contract was soon to be signed, that our street was expanding, and that The Hovel would be no more.

Not the way we had come to know it.

This troubled us, more than we liked to admit. Abandoned to its fate, The Hovel had become a point of anchor, a reminder of a state of deterioration we couldn't allow ourselves to reach. It had gained a shared value to us all, and by then, we were reluctant to give the house up to just anyone.

No matter, the buyers gave us six months to prepare for their arrival. It wasn't much, considering the extent of the work to be done on the house. At the time, however, we thought it was too long a wait since, for most of those six months, the buyers kept to themselves, and we were unable to claim our rights.

The husband came occasionally, did a whole survey of the construction, then left without acknowledging us. The woman, his wife, was there quite often and stayed longer too. Sometimes she brought a gardener with her, other times she was accompanied by her young daughter. As the two of them lingered in the front garden, debating over what flowers to plant and where, we wondered if their silence was meant

to tease us, force us to take the first step, and surrender our sense of propriety.

And we did.

One day, deeming she had done enough waiting, Lise leaned over their fence and introduced herself. It turned out the woman was a foreigner. South American, although she looked European: a mixture of Spanish and Italian. This explained the whole team of South Americans the contractor had brought with him. *Different countries*, the woman observed, but we couldn't tell the difference.

Her name was Monica. She was very pleased with the work done.

"Then I'm happy for you," Lise said.

There wasn't much else she could find out, Monica suggesting by subtle backward steps that she had more pressing matters to attend to. The interaction was more than brief, but it served as a temporary balm.

Then came the day, at last. The moving trucks parked themselves in front of The Hovel, and we looked out of our windows with nervous expectation, waiting for the whole family to appear. The shiny black car arrived some minutes later.

It was just her and the girl.

3

On the day of the housewarming, The Hovel greeted us with undeniable pride, and a bit of relief as well. It was clear that a lot of thought had gone into each detail – from the colour on the walls to the texture of the lampshades – the house's aesthetic value increasing far above any of our own homes.

"The advantages of starting from scratch," Lise pointed out.

She thought it was just as commendable to make do with what was already there, and it was a valid observation, but none of our attempts to transform The Hovel could have exuded the confidence and ease (and money?) of Monica's idiosyncratic taste.

We tried moving the conversation to a more comfortable terrain. Rob urged Monica to describe the before and after of the renovations, lingering over technical details – the material for the new windows, the composition of the walls – when what we actually wanted to know was where in the world she got the idea to place a giant cactus in the middle of the living room.

"It's magnificent," Flo said, all the while reminding herself it wouldn't go with the decor of her no. 7.

Monica restricted the tour of the house to the ground floor. The choice was understandable, but it did make one wonder what might be lurking, hidden away upstairs. Could there be something in her bedroom that, absolutely ordinary to the eyes of an outsider, held a personal significance she wished to shelter from us?

Flo liked to give people the benefit of the doubt: innocent until proven guilty, and all that other positive psychology she had been honing ever since the birth of her twins. She thought of the alarm clock on her nightstand, which had stopped working years before. She couldn't say why she refused to get rid of it, but occasionally she moved its hands to match the time on her watch, hoping this gesture would return some relevance to the clock. Why couldn't Monica have her own useless clock?

After scanning the living room one last time, we moved on to the kitchen. Monica proudly described it as the hidden gem of the house, so we looked around: at the large black marble island in the centre, the oven and cooker, and so on. We could see why she would love it now, but what had she seen in it before?

"None of the other houses I visited had such a spacious kitchen," Monica stated.

The room, stripped down to its very bones, could

have potential but, in our opinion, the added elements were what made it valuable. Grossly assessing the amount of that value, we were inclined to ask in what capacity Monica cooked.

"I've some professional experience, but I chose not to pursue that line of work."

A soft *hmm* issued from our lips.

"It's a demanding career," Flo granted.

"Oh, that wasn't the problem."

She opened the fridge, pulled out a bottle of white wine, and made sure all of us had a full glass in our hands before the conversation could continue. We made a mental note of her polite dismissal then turned to the different canapés served across her counter.

"You must have noticed the school," Fran said by way of introduction. "I live right beside it, at no. 11, and work there too. We're all very proud of it."

"How much does the school pay you to say that?"

Monica laughed after saying this, so we did too, taking a bite out of those curious pasties she said were her country's speciality. They were an instant crowd-pleaser; and whether it was the combination of flavours or the delicate pattern of the folded pastry, they helped numb an uncomfortable truth: we couldn't make sense of her kind of irony.

"What will you do for the rest of the summer?" Rob asked.

"We're staying put."

"Sound choice after a move."

"Yes, it'll give us time to explore the neighbourhood properly."

We nodded, hoping she would explain who was included in that *us*. After all, we had seen a couple visiting the house; and if that man was the daughter's father, then why weren't we meeting him? We failed to ask this, however, finding ourselves unable to come up with the adequate words to express our concern. LV wasn't a neighbourhood one wanted to explore alone, and perhaps it was best if she allowed us to guide her.

Sipping the last drop of wine in her glass, Fran studied her new neighbour. Monica was standing tall, her hands holding on to the edge of the island – not exactly resting on it for support, but pushing firmly against it. Fran wouldn't have said this posture frightened her, but it certainly didn't put her at ease. We thought we were observing Monica, but perhaps this was what she wanted us to believe. Inside The Hovel, we were under her authority; and the more she praised the various assets of the house, the closer she came to have us admit we had been completely mistaken in our original judgement of The Hovel.

As we lingered there, saying *well* multiple times without really departing, Monica directed her attention to the large window beside her – or rather, to the man who could be seen through that window. Her right-hand-side neighbour was entering his home, grocery bags in hand, looking somewhat scruffy. She told us she hadn't met him yet and wondered why he hadn't accepted her invitation.

"Clearly, he has nothing better to do."

This might have been a clever time for us to tell her it was natural of him, that he never participated in any of the activities of the neighbourhood, and that he would most likely ignore her at every chance he got. A warning might have saved us many future quandaries.

Instead, we just said: "That's Mr Martin."

"Same surname – but not a relation of ours," Anne added, pointing to both Lise and herself.

Monica paused, then smiled.

"I am surrounded."

We laughed once again, though unsure what she meant. Should we be offended? Lise was still intent on building good relations, so she thought it best to ignore this and thank Monica for having improved the status of our street with the lovely work she had done to the house.

"It seems that the title of 'hovel' can now be transferred to Mr Martin's house."

It was intended as a throwaway comment, but then we turned to the right and studied the house in question. Lise was making a good point. Whereas The Hovel, no. 8, had risen and gained aesthetic value, Mr Martin's house, no. 6, had proportionately declined.

It was only on that day, and through this comparison, that we became aware of their intricate connection. Sister houses, they had been – supporting each other in their unfavourableness, making up their own form of resistance. If our memories were correct, they had been built around the same time.

Would it be preposterous to think they had chosen to decline together? Now no. 8 was abandoning its Sister for better prospects, and the latter was starting to act up. How hadn't we noticed before the mouldy stain that appeared right beneath no. 6's roof, spreading downwards as the neat paintwork of The Hovel received its final touches?

"Well," Rob joked, "he might be tempted to call Monica for advice."

And on this note, we gathered our things and left.

That same night, when Lise looked at the plain white paper of the invitation and the neat handwriting in black, she found she could recognise in those details the woman who had sent it. Did this mean she had successfully moved one step closer to her? The thought pleased her, and she resolved to say something about it to Anne the next day.

4

Anne didn't know what to say.

If she were truly honest, Anne would tell her sister she was getting it all wrong: our position in regard to Monica hadn't progressed but remained very much on unstable grounds. In fact, it might have worsened. Until this first interaction, Monica had been a perfect stranger and could therefore be treated as such. Now she was an acquaintance who showed no clear signs of warming up to us. There was still some margin for progression, but if we hoped Monica would become one of us, we would have to rethink our approach.

It was all a matter of adaptation.

Anne knew this because, years before, she had to ask herself how best to survive in a society like LV, when she had no interest in sharing every second of her time with others. It had nothing to do with misanthropy. Anne had her friends, her regular lovers. And it wasn't egotism either, but something close to self-preservation. The idea of people in itself didn't repulse her; it was adapting her behaviour to a social circle that caused her anxiety. She liked having a taste of it, but only with the option of taking a step back whenever she needed to.

For a while, she tried living in the capital, thinking the city would make it much easier to go about unnoticed; and it did, but there were still times when Anne needed a little bit of company. So, she analysed the select people in her life and realised there was only her family she could potentially share a house with: who else could she bluntly tell to leave her alone without them feeling insulted?

Returning to the suburbs proved to be the best compromise for the lifestyle she wished to lead. LV, and our street, acted as a bulky presence, a background noise that made her feel safe, accompanied, and which she could face as one.

If we didn't object to her return, it was because she represented no real force of opposition. Anne thought of herself as the rebel cell, but she had been reared in our street, nurtured by LV – there were deep LV-ian instincts she couldn't shake off. Besides, she proved useful in taking care of the elder Martins, her parents, who could no longer live in that big house by themselves.

But her return did come with a small price. Anne had lived new experiences and she noticed, through comparison with her city friends, that we all suffered from the same condition: a distinctive lack of decisiveness.

It was this indecision that had us all converge

towards LV in the first place, convinced that the suburbs were a decent trade: halfway between the promise of open spaces and the pull of hectic crowds. This arrangement, however, didn't relieve our condition. Rather, we became hyper-aware of the two lifestyles we could potentially adopt, drifting between city or country life, never able to find a balance. The city, by its immediate vicinity, prevailed at uncertain times and this manifested itself in our fickle relationship with nature.

We cared deeply for the neat line of trees on the main boulevard, smiled gently at the ducks and swans in their artificial lake. Sunday walks around the park were a staple of LV life: parents and strollers, pensioners and dogs, allowing themselves one hour of nature friendliness. Yes, LV provided us with fresh air and large spaces, but the vibration of wheels on asphalt from the city followed us into our beds. And in that landscape of red-tile roofs and blue skies hovered a dusty and corroded cloud that concealed the horizon.

This clash of elements made us fidgety, unable to stay outside for too long without some source of distraction. Those of us with green thumbs did the minimum necessary to keep the garden looking alive, while our children played ball for a few minutes, only to return to the comfort of their rooms and the consolation of their video games. Only the elder Martins spent hours tending to their garden, taking pride in winning the council's Garden of the Year award year after year, but that was just a generational thing.

We thought this indecision was inevitable, that suffering from it was a necessary condition to reside in LV – that is, until *they* arrived.

Monica and the girl didn't react to it. They didn't even seem to acknowledge the potential risk, the danger of ever developing a similar condition. Whenever a bit of sunshine pierced through the dusty cloud, they ran outside and tended to their flowers, read on sun-loungers, or played with their dog. Walking from the school, we could see parts of their garden, and there would always be the shadow of a moving body on the lawn. How was it they preserved such rosy cheeks and a honey glaze to their complexion that was more appropriate to a summer spent on the coast than a life of urbanity?

Without properly understanding why this confused us, we would study their features and resent the complacency they represented. This reaction was what kept Anne from telling her sister what she really thought of our new neighbours. She had understood that only a body truly resistant to our indecision could display those features.

And why would a resistant body ever feel the need to adapt?

5

With one pale hand holding the straps of her basket, Fran closed the door to her house and made for the market. Passing the school, she heard a buzzing sound. It came from far behind, following her – closer, louder, then right in front of her.

It was Monica's girl, riding her scooter. She reached the end of the street, turned, and with a brisk *hello* pushed off from the ground, propelling herself forward. Fran shook her head. A bright blue helmet but no elbow pads. Was anyone watching her? The scooter glided away, gleaming under the soft light of the Sunday sun, and Fran felt a sudden urge to scold her son for staying inside. But a scolding wouldn't make Alex develop a desire for sunshine, so she turned her back to the girl and walked in the opposite direction.

She was heading to the market later than usual and feared the best produce would be snatched up. Upon arrival, however, Fran soon lost interest in the state and quality of her favourite peaches. There were greater reasons for concern. Two, to be precise.

It was beside the dairy stand that Jo, no. 9, first established contact with Monica. Jo hadn't been in town on the day of the housewarming, and she was now hunting for information. She could have come to us for details, but as with many other aspects of her life, she had preferred taking matters into her own hands. There was nothing inherently wrong about Jo's actions but for the choice of hunting in plain sight. And at the Sunday market, of all places.

Hovering beside the line at the fruit stand, Fran inched away from the person in front of her and moved closer to them.

"… but it's the same everywhere else, I guess. And how did you come to choose *this* town, anyway?"

"Someone I knew used to live here."

"They don't anymore?"

"No, they do… but we've had a falling out."

There followed a moment of silence where Fran officially detached herself from the line and Jo waited for Monica to develop this last comment. But it seemed it wasn't to be so, and the thought slipped away. Jo could have pried even further, if she hadn't noticed Fran standing at such close range. Instead, she took a step back, and Monica instinctively moved with her.

This gesture revealed part of Jo's intentions.

On that same morning, while the girl asked if she could ride her scooter outside and Fran planned the week ahead of her, Jo had awakened with the conviction that Monica's arrival was her call to action.

Here was the perfect opportunity to slip away from us, slowly, then all at once. First, however, she slipped out of bed, made herself a speedy breakfast, then dressed with assurance: her blue cardigan left unbuttoned over her shirt and her belt buckled up tight. Then out she went, intending to buy only one thing at the market: Monica's confidence.

This awakening hadn't come as suddenly as we wanted to believe. It had been ripening for quite some time; rotting, perhaps, from too long a wait. For many years we'd maintained a friendly relationship with Jo – not close, but of mutual tolerance. Then, one day, her status changed, throwing us into disarray. Was being left by a husband she despised a silver lining? Without an answer, we were unable to determine whether she wanted to be consoled or not; and seeing that this awkwardness was increasing with every new attempt at a conversation, we decided respectful silence was the safest way to go.

As the months passed, Jo closed herself off, tethered to the wisteria shrubs of her front porch. She invited friends from outside of LV and only came out to pick up the boy she tutored after school hours. We came to think that the only reason she stayed in LV was for the sheer stubbornness of not giving up the house – her spot in the street – without a fight. We respected her for that.

We did realise our silence wasn't the best method to express our sympathies, but by then a sudden change in our behaviour would be misconstrued as pity, and that wasn't an emotion we wanted in our street. Pity is a perverted form of empathy. Haven't we all experienced at least once the humiliation that comes from excessive smiling, higher-pitched greetings, and tilted heads? The person on the receiving end always shrinking under the judgement, never finding any benefit from it.

In the end, it was because we cared for our community that we stuck to our initial strategy: if we pretended that nothing had happened, that no one had left, our street would remain one whole, complete puzzle.

Truth be told, we had also preferred *him*, Jo's husband. He was of a simpler build, congenial, and prone to share funny anecdotes. Jo, on the other hand, could make us feel uncomfortable, insisting on using only self-deprecating humour. Our feelings towards her could have been more clearly defined had there been something specific for which we could resent her.

Jo, then, had valid reasons for wanting to sever our ties, and with this conviction in mind, she walked up to the market that day, her head held high. She even went so far as breaching the gap of physical contact and rested a hand on Monica's shoulder when laughing over the anecdote of the wild cat she had once owned.

Fran still remembered the shade of arrogance Monica had shown at her housewarming, and as she handed the merchant the money for a quarter of brie, a sharp tingling in her spine caused her to stare over her shoulder at the two women. It was natural for Jo to show some restraint in front of us, but if Monica displayed a similar propensity, was it safe to let them act as catalysts to each other? Her inkling wasn't unfounded, but she would need proof to debate it with the rest of us, so Fran summoned up the courage to intervene, marching straight over and asking:

"Ladies! How are you doing on this fine day?"

"All good," Monica replied with a smile.

Jo mirrored the sentiment with a simple nod.

"Goodbye summer and hello routine, right?"

Jo tilted her head, not meeting her eyes.

"Monica, your little one is starting a new school, it's exciting!"

"She's a bit worried, but yes, mostly excited."

"She must be in the same class as my Alex. They're the same age if I'm correct? Don't worry, I'll ask him to keep an eye on her."

"They're the same age, yes, but Emilia is going to another school. The International School, in SG. They have a bilingual programme there."

Jo's eyes returned to the conversation. It had been many years since she had been personally involved with matters of the school, but she remembered what our standards were. Monica's choice would be received as a serious blow; and it was at this precise moment she felt convinced of her morning's awakening.

Fran put her wallet back inside her purse, taking a moment to think of something appropriate to say. Monica's decision was understandable, nevertheless she pondered over its legitimacy. No contract stipulated the girl *had* to attend our school simply because she lived on our street; but going as far as to choose *SG*, of all other towns! Here it was, clear as day – Fran's instinct never failed. Still, it was much too early to arrive at a verdict on Monica, so she avoided commenting on the matter by inviting her daughter to Alex's birthday party.

"That way she can meet some of the children in the neighbourhood."

"That's very nice of you! She'll be thrilled."

With a final nod, the group broke apart, Monica and Jo walking back together.

Fran was certain Jo would be invited inside The Hovel. What would she think of the giant cactus?

6

It seemed to us that the match was… peculiar, to say the least. And yet it persisted, with numerous invitations for coffee and spontaneous calls as one of the two walked past the other's house.

For all the confidence she displayed in front of us, Monica might have sensed that resisting the comfort of Jo's extended hand wasn't a luxury she could afford. The friendship could very well be genuine, although to us it seemed that, above all, they were using each other as buffers against us. The thought was unsettling.

Would Monica have reconsidered her choice of an ally if she had known the poisonous seed her new friend would plant inside her mind?

We know Jo hadn't done it intentionally and would later blame herself for the role she played in what was to unfold. At first, she had simply responded to a comment Monica made about her direct neighbour: this curious habit of appearing out of nowhere in his garden and disappearing just as furtively seconds later.

"Mr Martin is one to watch, for sure," Jo said.

Sensing the thankful validation Monica felt upon hearing this, Jo continued and expanded her criticism over "the old man." Jo knew strong alliances needed a common target; and though we were clearly the final one, agreeing on a system of resistance, and going against our street as a whole, was a task that could take weeks, perhaps months. She needed something quicker, short-term. Something that would secure the first link to Monica.

It was a lapse in judgement. Jo had never been directly affected by the presence of Mr Martin, not more than the rest of us, but he was the easiest target, that one solid link. She couldn't have known that the ground on which she was planting that seed was so uncommonly fertile.

It had been tilled during the many hours Monica spent alone in her house, breathing in the pernicious atmosphere of The Hovel. Watching through her window, perhaps one too many times. We knew some of those hours were dedicated to her translation works, which had evidently supplanted her mysterious cooking career, but was that intellectual exercise enough to fill the void?

That comment from Jo, a mere push, couldn't have caused such a rapid fall.

In the end, the jump was deliberate.

PART TWO

A SHIFTING OF ENERGIES

Any and all living spaces, from the quaint hamlet in the provinces to the Neoclassical buildings in the heart of the city, have their own distinctive energies. Extremely fragile, the energies make up the unity of these different spaces.

The people living in them like to think they are the ones defining this energy, that it is their uniqueness which makes the energy what it is. But they fail to see the larger picture. They fail to see that if they were drawn to this space, it's because they were a perfect match. Like a blood type, they can only survive if the combination allows it. And just like a blood type, they can spend an entire life not knowing, never wondering, why this energy and not another.

In the leagues of residential towns, floral suburbia, with none of the aristocratic airs of an SG or a V but entitled enough to create an *oh* as a response to its name, LV didn't escape this rule. Although it did have one specific feature: its inhabitants were of the hypochondriac type, convinced that LV's energy, this inherent quality they didn't fully comprehend, was fragile and needed to be preserved.

It is what made our immune system so responsive. It was efficient in dealing with any strange mix, driving the intruder away before it could cause any severe harm. Which is why it made no sense that Monica should have survived so long among us.

Her energy was other; not necessarily corrosive in its absolute form but detrimental, in the long run, to our well-being. Trapped in her magnetic aura, we began to develop uncharacteristic behaviours, patterns we later identified as side effects. Like an infection, of sorts, from prolonged exposure. It took us many months to realise this behaviour wasn't normal. Several more to understand it. Clarity came sporadically, when we moved out of The Hovel's range and the beating against our temples softened, becoming no more than the tranquil drumming of a healthy heart.

The facts were simple. Our energy was being subverted.

In her own way, Monica too suffered from her infectious state. Not being surrounded by like-minded souls intensified her distress, her daughter Emilia being still too young to offer any kind of support. She had to fight our system's response alone and often doubled the intensity of her attacks. These bouts of Fever would develop randomly, unexpectedly. We rarely knew what caused them.

1

The first outburst of her Fever happened on the day of the power cut.

It was the children's first school play. A Saturday evening in autumn, with its distinctive bleakness and early sunset. Clouds had crowded over our street toward midday. We were gathered in the main hall of the school, performers and spectators alike, when the first drops of rain began to fall. The forecast that morning had mentioned rain, but it had not prepared us for the wind that began blowing.

Unexpected and violent, the wind picked up as the children closed the first act and the curtain fell. The windows in the hall rattled, causing a few boys on the stage to lose focus. Between lines, they uttered tiny yelps and giggled to attract attention, or hide the fact they were truly terrified. Their parents smiled encouragingly, holding up their phones and video cameras. The elder siblings distracted themselves by crudely grading the performance of each child. We decided to ignore the storm, hidden as we were behind the opaque windows of the building. In the warmth of the overheated hall, we couldn't imagine that the rain beating against the glass was ice-cold.

Then the moment we had all been waiting for arrived, when the children gathered on the stage for the final song. A still peacefulness settled as a little blond girl from the front row took a step forward. She was prepared to hit her high note, encouraged by the prospect of future praise and applause. She opened her lips, but as the air from her lungs pushed up and touched the vocal cords, the hall turned dark.

Paralysed by confusion, we merely watched as our children shrieked. The principal was the only one to act. He turned on his flash-light and stepped onstage.

"Children, be calm! Stay where you are. Your parents will come and get you!"

To this cue, we all moved at once, bumping into each other, not knowing where to go. Some of us grabbed the arm of the wrong child and only noticed our mistake when, trying to calm down said child, the light of our phones flashed on their whimpering faces.

Flo was at the back, both hands tight on the shoulders of her twins. She was disoriented and preferred waiting until the hall was clear. As she stood there, she witnessed in shame how some parents lingered around the food table, taking back the quiches and pastries they had brought; how some rogue teenagers were gulping down the red wine strictly reserved for the adults, red-tainted lips grinning. Her twins fidgeted under the pressure of her hands. The principal approached her, saying something about a power cut, how it must have come from somewhere else in the street since all was in order here. Flo stared back, blankly.

"Oh, apologies, in the darkness you looked just like Fran," the principal fumbled. "Well… why don't you go back to your house? Check if the power's out there too."

Flo hesitated: "What happened?"

"Just the storm."

Except this was a wrongful accusation. The storm had only played with the trees, tickling their branches until one of them snapped. How could it have known that this one branch would take in its fall the wires from the electrical pole beside it? The branch now lay limp on the ground, harmless, while the stray wires dangled menacingly in the air above it; and as the storm receded, the accusation against it was lifted. It was the provenance of said branch that mattered to us most: the tree from which it snapped, and the plot on which it stood.

The next morning, when Flo entered her kitchen to make breakfast for her children, she noticed some of us gathering outside no. 6: Mr Martin's. Immediately alerted, she left the coffee brewing in the pot and rushed outside. She made a beeline towards Lise who, in her opinion, was the one most likely to know what was afoot.

"He should have pruned that tree," Lise snapped. "It's grown excessively these past few months, and with the wires and everything so close to it…"

A few steps behind Lise, Monica and Jo were whispering. Their gestures were agitated, tense, and they kept pointing to no. 6 and its trees. Flo eyed them curiously and was tempted to approach, but Lise had more to say.

"The electrical company says it'll still be a few hours before they can come."

Rob confirmed this: "They said it would most likely be in the evening."

There was nothing else to do but disperse and wait, and for this Flo was summoned to Lise's house for coffee. As she followed, Flo noticed Monica remained standing, studying the maimed tree, and she felt she ought to say something – anything at all. *Would she care to join them?*

"Where is he?" Monica asked.

"Excuse me?"

"Mr Martin, has anyone seen him?"

Lise jumped in: "Rob saw him leaving in his car earlier."

"Of course… what a coward."

Flo and Lise agreed, but the sharpness of her tongue surprised them. They whispered *well* to each other and, without a moment's hesitation, turned around, not waiting to see if Monica accepted the invitation. After all, she mightn't have heard, or pretended she hadn't, because she too walked away, muttering some Spanish words in form of farewell.

2

In those powerless circumstances, we separated into two groups: those who were staying, and those going to the city where electricity was still abundant.

For those of us who stayed, it was back to old forms of entertainment. Could we remember the rules to card games we hadn't played in years? Significant time passed before we came to an agreement and decided on the correct regulations, but, eventually, we found ourselves enjoying the games and mindless chat in between shuffles. By the end of the day, our nerves had been soothed to such a degree that, when the power returned, we forgot about the food that had gone to waste, the misuse of expensive scented candles, or the possible damage to hard drives. The incident became a funny little anecdote, marking the start of the autumn break.

What none of us expected, however, was that Monica would be of a very different mind. The following week, she came to us with a letter she had drafted herself, on behalf of us all, and addressed to the council at the town hall. She detailed the events of the weekend, demanding the council act immediately: Mr Martin was at fault, and he should take responsibility.

The letter was passed around and corrected on some points of thought and wording (common mistakes among non-natives). We agreed with her on the premise of the appeal but confessed we found it peculiar she should have mentioned the school play (which she hadn't attended) and called Mr Martin *uncooperative*, as that suggested there had been preliminary requests on our part – a gross exaggeration. And was it really necessary to contact the council? Incidents of this scale were typically handled by the veterans of the street. Whether or not Monica acknowledged this unspoken rule (and it seemed she knew *exactly* what she was doing), we insisted that the problem be fixed internally, like the cordial neighbours we were.

"But," Monica protested, "Mr Martin's been *avoiding us since Saturday!*"

"Has he?" Flo distinctly remembered no one had looked around for him.

"I've rung his doorbell a few times, and he never answers."

"That isn't really out of character," Fran argued.

"So we should just accept it?"

Yes, that was precisely what we wanted to do, but Monica wouldn't let the matter go, so we sighed and agreed to sign her letter.

Weeks passed without any response from the

council, a silence we had anticipated. The council must have read the letter, perhaps they had even considered pleasing the newcomer to prove to her the council was efficient and legitimate; but ultimately, they decided against disrupting the natural order of our street. Monica would be disappointed; however, this was a valuable lesson for her.

At least, this was our over-confident reading of events.

The reality was that the council had chosen to contact Mr Martin directly, yet another circumvention of our carefully constructed network. We realised our mistake when the old man emerged from his house to open the gates for the pruning team. He would never have done so of his own volition.

We waited for him to comment on our letter, but he responded with silence. Did he even know there had been one? He didn't try apologising to us for the trouble caused by his wildly overgrown tree either. What he did was go over to Monica's house and ask if she wanted the team to prune any of the trees that were crowning over her garden.

Jo had dropped in for a chat when Mr Martin rang. She watched from the kitchen as the two neighbours went to the back garden, studied each tree, and chose which ones would be cut. Jo had to resist the urge to join them and stand there, firm, supporting her friend. It wouldn't do any good. The old man barely acknowledged Jo's existence, no matter how firm she stood, and his insipid reaction would only upset her more. But he did seem to respond to

Monica's presence. Jo wouldn't say he was hunched, exactly. Rather, there seemed to be a diminishment of his persona, as if Monica's assertive stance was foiling an instinctive masculine authority.

"He was all smiles," she told Jo after he had left. "Quite the charmer, actually. I can imagine what type of man he must've been in his youth. Reminds me of my brother…" she trailed off. "But that smile doesn't fool me! I know exactly how to deal with *his* type."

Jo hadn't realised there was even a type to look for in the old man. Perhaps his peculiar 'charm' relied on the tone and quality of his elocution; and, in all her years living on our street, she had barely heard him speak. Jo let the thought linger, feeling that a question was forming inside her brain, but not quite sure what she wanted to know.

"… and my letter was a success after all! I knew the council wouldn't ignore me if I mentioned the school. That's how things work in this world, a threat with a veneer of formality."

So this wasn't Monica's first neighbourhood dispute.

"Now the garden looks clean and I spent no extra money."

Jo was impressed by the thoroughness of the approach, but she was also a tad disappointed. Part of her had wanted Monica's Fever to be the driving force behind this new win, but, once again, a mere calculated move controlled the odds. She wasn't sure why she felt this way. It could simply be that

Jo had reached a point in her community life where she expected her neighbours to entertain her. Lately, nothing amused her more than watching us buzzing and squirming at each unexpected move Monica made.

3

We had never dwelled too long on the life of Mr
Martin.

The majority of us met him when he had already
developed his habit of reclusion. We accepted it
without question. This wasn't to say we felt no
curiosity. Every so often, we were nagged by a few
probing questions, and we shared these with each
other. After some time, we had managed to piece
together a rather disjointed puzzle of his story, but
one that satisfied us enough to live with: we knew he
had attended one of the most prestigious business
schools in the city, married soon after and had two
children. At some point, his wife left, taking the children with her. We never learned why.

It was quite possible Mr Martin was aware of the
interest he sparked, which led us to think that if he
started avoiding us, it wasn't out of dislike, or hatred,
but out of *fear*. Fear of an interrogation. Without
any greater stimulation from the prime source, our
curiosity soon waned, and we let the matter go.

Monica was still at that first, curious level, and it soon became clear she was intent on climbing even higher. In the weeks that followed the power cut, she used every encounter with us as an opportunity to collect information. She would throw into the conversation a comment that would poke at our scant knowledge of Mr Martin, until a piece of the story fell into her hands. Generally, she used his house as a starting point. When exactly had he stopped taking care of it? When had he planted those large bushes in the front?

"He really searched for the most tenacious species. This jungle of his, it's resisting winter quite well."

We too had noticed this. The trees on his front garden were holding on to their decaying leaves — "shielding him from view," as Monica had put it — while our oak trees were soon to be completely bare. And yet, our instinct was to protect him, and we tried to justify the old man's need for privacy, calling to his freedom of speech, or lack thereof. Every time we did so, however, we exposed new details. Until, finally, Monica had the same exact picture it had taken us years to assemble.

But still, she wasn't satisfied. She was convinced there was more to his story, an element we had overlooked or were unable to get to; and having exhausted our knowledge, she turned to another source.

We couldn't figure out when she made the connection, understanding that the ones who knew Mr Martin the longest were the other Martins, the seniors. They lived in the guesthouse at the back of Anne's terrain – *their* terrain, originally, though kindly given to their youngest daughter when she decided to return to LV. The main house was too big for them, anyway. They moved out willingly, knowing that their old age had indeed made them guests now: welcome to stay, but only for as long as nature saw fit.

From the large windows of her house, Monica could no doubt see the elder Martins – especially Mrs Martin, who, despite her bad hip, spent many rainless days tending to her prize-winning garden. If she and Monica passed each other, say, on the way to the bakery, they would smile and say hello, but nothing further. They had yet to sit down for a proper conversation.

That was until December came along, and Anne decided she would like to throw a small get-together for her birthday.

4

Turning forty wasn't a regular event, so Anne figured she deserved to act with a dash of self-centredness. Why shouldn't she have her cousins take a three-hour-long drive just to wish her a happy birthday?

With Christmas being so close to the date, she usually opted against a proper celebration. It was foolish to have the whole family travel twice – and better, for her, to save patience for the holidays. Just this once, however, Anne felt she had enough energy to brave the crowd twice. It was a first symptom of her exposure to Monica's energy, a failure of our system, but she didn't know it yet and went along with it, sending out invitations to her entire family and, without awaiting a response, starting to plan the event.

Yet what about us, her dear old neighbours? She hesitated, considering. Yes, she could include us as well. It would be less awkward, certainly, than to have us witness the merriment from afar. The larger the crowd, the less she would be expected to engage with every guest individually. We might act as buffers against the crowd, and she could have her peace.

When the night came, however, our task wasn't as easily achieved as we'd thought. Having introduced ourselves to the other members of the Martin family, we attempted to join their conversation but were unable to understand their private language, made of memories and inside jokes. Defeated, we slipped away and gathered in a corner of the room to talk among ourselves. From our safe distance, we watched Anne sway from one guest to another, sighing whenever she caught our gaze.

She could have been entirely dissatisfied if Monica and her daughter hadn't then arrived. More than an hour after the specified seven p.m., but just in time to provide some much-needed distraction. Monica eyed us standing in our corner, glasses and canapés in hand, and hesitated. She scanned the room, landing at its centre, where, seated on the couch and helping themselves to the snacks on the coffee table, she found the elder Martins.

"She came for *them*," Lise whispered to Anne.

Anne ignored her sister and went to greet the new arrivals, arms extended. Monica accepted the embrace. After all, it was quite the positive gesture, a bit unlike Anne but much to her guest's taste. And they had brought a present! Anne thanked them but didn't open it. Naturally, she was keen to see what was inside; but as with the other gifts, she preferred opening them in the privacy of her room, where she could properly assess each gift in terms of quality, value, and originality. Delaying opening time was a guarantee she wouldn't have to fake a reaction. It would also be a cause for celebration after everyone had gone. These assurances made it easier to face the crowd, and so Anne set down the gift with the others, proud of her towering pile.

For the rest of that night, Monica's present, this mystery box wrapped in fancy cream-coloured paper and a bow to match, was a taunt.

Anne never shared with the rest of us what was inside.

When this welcoming ritual came to an end, Emilia scurried away to join the group of children playing in the back garden, freeing her mother's arm, which Anne snatched. She was determined to sit Monica down next to her parents. Anne had heard the rumours of Monica's interest in the old man, but she had never been subjected to an interrogation herself. She wanted to see what the fuss was all about. Her parents were too tired to move around the crowded room, but their memories were perfectly intact. If Monica so desired, and no one came to interrupt them, she could ask all the questions she wanted. Would their answers finally satisfy her?

Monica followed the hostess without objection, nodding vaguely at Lise when meeting her eyes. Lise responded in kind, then turned around to pour herself a glass of wine. Although her sister might have no qualms in surrendering her parents as prey, Lise thought it wiser to keep her ears pricked and her feet close to the couch. If she then started walking from one relative to the other, it was only to achieve what she thought was a subtle diversion. Occasionally, she stopped to talk to us, and it was through her coordinated efforts that new information about Emilia's father was uncovered: how the pair had recently got divorced and, him travelling regularly, they had decided Emilia should live with Monica. They were spending the coming holidays with *his* family, for the sake of the girl and taking into account Monica's family, who lived on a different continent.

"Don't you miss home, darling?" Mrs Martin asked Monica.

She tilted her head from one side to the other.

"There's not much of a home left to miss."

When this comment eventually reached us, Fran placed a hand on her heart and re-evaluated, for a second, her prior judgement of Monica. We urged her, however, not to look at the woman with those pitiful eyes, and, with no firm object to hold onto, the compassion vanished just as easily as it had come. Still, we waited eagerly for more information, not entirely sure what we were hoping to hear: if it was general knowledge that could take us closer to the woman's inner self, or specific facts we could use in later interactions. Facts that would give us the upper hand.

"It seems we've been here forever," Mrs Martin said, changing the subject to something less intimate. "The girls were teenagers. And we moved around the country quite a lot before that, but LV is where we decided to settle."

"So, all the other residents… you must've seen them coming, one at a time."

"Yes, I guess we are long-standing witnesses."

"And you knew the previous owners of my house, then? I heard they were a peculiar family."

Lise, passing canapés, saw Monica's eyes light up and her neck stretch forward. Alarmed, she dodged two hungry uncles and bolted to the centre of the room, giving up any sense of grace or subtlety. She stood behind the couch, very still, careful not to miss a single word.

"Peculiar is a nice way of putting it," the father said, perfectly aware of where Monica was taking the conversation, but very much amused by the situation. "For some reason, our street attracts… *odd birds*."

With only a vague idea of who her father was grouping under that denomination, Lise chose not to communicate this comment to us; and yet a pause in the general conversation, combined with the acoustics of the room, allowed the words to travel all the way to our corner.

"But as for knowing them," he went on. "They kept to themselves. Which was a surprise, given their *eccentric* nature."

"A bit like our namesake," Mrs Martin added.

At this moment, our informant was summoned away from the room by one of her cousins, who needed her help with the retelling of an anecdote Lise had witnessed. A long moment of silence followed, where bits and pieces of the conversation were lost. Then Lise finally returned to her post.

"We thought it very clever you should contact the council. We told our daughters to do it many times before, but they refused."

Lise pursed her lips. That wasn't exactly true. There had been suggestions of letters but never any adamant request from her parents. If anything had been said, it usually concerned The Hovel – Mr Martin's house was then included in the criticism but only in relation to its Sister. And yet, could it be that Lise had underestimated her parents' hostility towards the old man?

She thought to ask Anne about it, but her sister was making it a point not to care about the subject. Although somewhat worrying, Monica's obsession wouldn't tarnish Anne's eagerness. This wasn't why she had planned the party. Besides, it would soon be time for cake, and would someone help her with the bottles of champagne?

5

Had we understood earlier how the Fever actually worked – what Monica could and couldn't control – we might have judged the entire matter differently. If we had only grasped the simpleness of the natural law of energies, we wouldn't have cared so much. Perhaps none of this would have happened. It was our eagerness to include her that turned against us. Our system kept trying to alert us: we weren't being firm enough with the law. Monica's energy was a clear mismatch.

As it was, we still wanted to believe in our individual ability to connect with her. Not all of us could be compatible with her personality, of course, but someone had to be. And yet the ratio was so low, if not non-existent, that we couldn't but be alarmed.

If we had to sum it up, our main difficulty when interacting with Monica lay in her tone: convivial and expressive at first, it would inadvertently drop to a dry note we could only interpret as sarcasm; and if she turned to the person next to us, the tone regained its conviviality, so that each of us thought she sounded friendlier when speaking to another.

Yet *something* had made it possible for her to connect with the elder Martins. Their exchange had run smoothly, Monica exuding a warmth she had never before shown to us; and she left the party with a look of utter contentment. After much consideration, we came up with three different explanations. The first one was that Monica's Fever had infected the old couple, and their sympathy towards her was but a symptom of this. Then, for a moment, we considered that the elder couple's energy could be other than what we had always believed; but the third option was much more likely: we were simply being fooled, and Monica, eager to have a piece of the Mr Martin puzzle we didn't yet possess, had manipulated the old couple's ageing minds into speaking openly.

Faced with this act of downright derision, we were in our right to counterattack. Or… we could wait for the moment she would slip down the ridge created by her tricks and lies. We chose the latter, sure that balance would restore itself naturally.

Only Lise was unsatisfied with this solution. It wasn't so much the complexity of the situation that troubled her but the idea that her parents had opened up to this stranger in a way they had never done with her.

"But you never ask, honey," her mother said when questioned.

"I shouldn't *have* to ask."

"Well, if you want my opinion, there are too many vultures on our street."

"Vultures?"

Her mother patted her on the cheek and turned her attention back to her flowers.

6

Any number of strangers left their mark upon the gravel of our sidewalks. There were the subtle footprints of those parking their cars then rushing to catch the train that would take them to the city; the firm steps of some simply intent on reaching the other end of the road; and there were longer trails, from other meandering souls.

Ours was a quiet street, quiet and reserved. Mind you, there was nothing in the aspect of these transient individuals that advised us against trusting their good nature. It was when the stranger stopped, watched, and lingered for a moment too long, that our suspicions were awakened.

When Flo realised twenty minutes had passed since the woman standing outside of Mr Martin's had first arrived, she wondered if it wasn't her duty (nay, *obligation*) to go out and ask what her business on our street was. Nothing specific in the woman's appearance suggested ill will. On the contrary, she was a nice woman to look at, with her hair pulled up neatly into a bun and a monochrome outfit that must have required some serious thought. It was the fact she should be there at all that troubled Flo. It wasn't uncommon for people to stop outside of no. 6 – most of the time, it was an errand boy, delivering a parcel – but as far as she could remember, there had never been someone *waiting* for him.

Besides, this woman was persistent. She rang the doorbell once, twice, still waiting for a response. As she did so, she stood on her tiptoes and leaned on the railings to try and catch a glimpse at a shadow, a flash, anything that could potentially be seen through the small windows of the house. Flo doubted she could discern anything. The white winter light found no reflective surface, only the voluminous darkness that reigned inside. Perhaps the old man simply wasn't home. The stranger's last attempt with the doorbell was tentative, and eventually, she walked away.

But she didn't leave our street. Instead, she moved in the direction of The Hovel and, once there, tried her luck with this other doorbell. Monica worked from home, Flo remembered. Could she have been paying attention to the stranger's movements as well? The door to The Hovel was answered quickly, confirming her suspicion. It was a relief: Flo thought of herself more as an observer than an active player and she was glad she could now delegate her responsibility.

She finished packing her briefcase, favourite pen and notebook neatly in line, tied her shoelaces, but her mind kept returning to the woman outside, so she decided to pop her head between the curtains one last time… They had vanished.

Flo looked about desperately for any sign of the woman, only to realise two shadows were looming outside her gate. When the doorbell rang, Flo let go of the curtains, caught red-handed, and hesitated before making her way down to open the door. She should have left for work already. Perhaps they would believe so. But the woman… this could be Flo's sole chance to know more. She opened the door.

They were standing calmly over her doormat, the stranger one step behind Monica. She was introduced as *a friend of Mr Martin.*

"She tells me she hasn't heard from him since – sorry, you said *before* the holidays?"

The stranger nodded. "Right," Monica continued. "Now, I just got back into town yesterday, but maybe you've seen him in the past few days, or even today?"

Flo stared blankly. Her first instinct was to ask, *friend?* But clearly, that wouldn't do. Then she realised they were implying Mr Martin was *missing, which startled her even more. She had never thought of him as the protagonist of that kind of story.*

"To be honest, Mr Martin isn't seen much outside of his house, so absent or not, I haven't really noticed a difference."

"Oh, that's alright," the friend said. "Thank you anyway."

She took a step back, ready to depart, but Monica stopped her, eyes severe. Flo froze. She looked at no. 6, then back at the friend, before adding: "Maybe I saw him last week? I'm not sure. My mind's a bit of a blur; I wouldn't rely on it."

Flo laughed nervously. The friend pulled out a phone from her purse, looked at the screen, then shoved it into the pocket of her coat.

"He usually calls back… but in any case, I'm sorry for the bother!"

"Oh? No, not at all!"

With one last shake of the head, the friend headed back toward the street, Monica following without a word.

When Flo drove away to work, some minutes later, she saw the two women again, entering The Hovel. It sure was polite of Monica to give this stranger so much of her time; but Flo also wondered if there wasn't something more to this act of benevolence. Something that could have been prompted, perhaps, by Monica's distressing curiosity. We knew little then of what caused the Fever to flare up.

Flo's fingers tapped anxiously on the steering wheel. She could very well be wrong and so decided not to tell us about the lady friend right away. Instead, she persisted in thinking that everything was fine: Mr Martin, safe and well, was probably still in his house, being his natural reclusive self. There was no point in broadcasting worries.

A week later, however, when a police car parked itself outside no. 6, Flo peeked again through the windows of her bedroom and knew, this time, she would have to tell us the whole story.

7

A police car wasn't something we often saw on our street, especially in the middle of the school day. When the children walked into the playground and saw the car with its blue lights, they thronged behind the school fence and looked at one another, shouting stories that would explain its presence there. The unusualness excited them, stirring their imaginations. Their parents, however, were less than pleased; and from our windows, we watched the scene unfold with apprehension.

Two policemen came out of the car. They rang Mr Martin's doorbell twice before the old man agreed to emerge. He was somewhere in the brush. He looked calm, at first, then their exchange grew a bit tense. Visibly reluctant, he agreed to let them through. The policemen followed him as he led them to the back entrance of the house. Their visit was extremely short, and when the policemen came out, their faces were streaked with confusion.

Mr Martin was upset by their intervention, though

not entirely abashed. He shook the men's hands and waited until their car turned around the corner to make his way to The Hovel. We all knew Monica was inside: the blinds were up, and the dog could be heard barking, vigorously, calling for his mistress's attention. She never answered the door.

We don't know how the information got to us, travelling haphazardly as information does, but a few days later we discovered that the police had received an anonymous call reporting suspicious activity at no. 6. It was then that Flo decided to let us know about her encounter with the *friend*. Returning home from work, she ran into Rob who told her the latest news about the incident. At first, Flo assumed the woman had never heard back from Mr Martin and, perhaps, decided to take matters into her own hands. But why call anonymously?

"Maybe she didn't want the old man to know it was her? In case her worries were unfounded," Rob suggested. He had time to think on the matter, Lise having called him at work the second the news broke out. "But it's a bold move."

Flo nodded, looking at The Hovel. She saw a silhouette moving in the living room. It was dark outside, and only one light was on in the house, so she couldn't tell if Monica could see them standing there.

"What if it wasn't the friend..." Flo finally said.

Rob nodded silently. Flo trusted his pragmatism, as well as his ability to keep things relatively quiet. He didn't need to follow Flo's gaze to understand

what she was suggesting.
    "Concern or spite?" he asked.
    "Let's hope for the best."

8

Days of hypotheses and debates led to the conclusion that Monica couldn't have made the call herself.
She was too smart to take such a risk – smarter still
to know just how to take advantage of this *friend*'s
worries and convince her to dial the number for the
police. Naturally, this conclusion spurred many more
questions, but no matter how we phrased them,
each version was too explicit in its accusation; and
because we felt uncomfortable letting Monica know
she had offended us, we kept silent.

And yet we couldn't let this offence go wholly
unpunished.

It was one thing to contact the council to arbi-
trate over neighbourly feuds. We had done it ourselves through the years: one street against another,
even numbers against uneven. The harmony of the
size and typography of the house numbers remains
a bone of contention. These arguments could create
animosity, but when it came it was short-lived, and
we laughed over it at the next Annual Gathering.

We respected the neighbour that confronted us, even more so if *they* won the battle.

Ultimately, the feuds made us aware of each other's concerns, so that the neighbourhood was made stronger with each obstacle surmounted.

Getting the police involved, however, was another matter entirely.

For one, it was an intrusion into our privacy. No external authority could truly understand the rules and customs of our street. Their intervention was demeaning; it claimed we were unable, or even too cowardly, to deal with a troublesome neighbour. And what, then, would other LV-ians think? *The Others*, as Anne had termed them. What, too, would all the other parents at our school think? Would they still feel their children, young and defenceless, were safe to spend most hours of the day on such an unstable street?

The balance kept tipping to Monica's side, and the shift of energy slowly began to stifle us. But not entirely, never to the point of passiveness. We understood now that we would have to create our own kind of disturbance if we wanted to avoid being caught in another outburst of her Fever.

It was no longer a question of restoring an original order but taking control of the overturned one. Mr Martin wasn't showing any symptoms yet, but the challenging atmosphere of the Sister Houses could very possibly have weakened his defences, and we needed to restore him to a more stable state. We decided, then, to build a safety net around him. This strategy relied on subtle gestures of concern and generosity. Small stones we could add to our pan to level the scales. To better watch him and keep him on check.

Rob, for instance, noticed Mr Martin was having trouble starting his car. This lack of mobility could be problematic, so he offered to check the engine and possibly fix it. The old man had no good reason to decline the offer, and one Saturday the two men pushed the car onto the road, spent a couple of hours working together, and even chatted. Mr Martin didn't question this new behaviour. He didn't even look surprised, as if he had implicitly agreed and submitted to the plan.

When they were done (or decided they were, neither of them really knowing much about cars), Rob invited him back to his house for a cold beer. Lise welcomed them gladly, although she thought Rob could have been sensible enough to go to Mr Martin's house instead.

"But this way other people can see we trust him enough to invite him into our own house, where our children are."

"Good point."

What Rob failed to mention was that he deliberately chose to avoid no. 6. It was the last place he wanted to visit, sensing there was something within he didn't want to see with his own eyes.

This was a biased perception, based on the old man's living habits, yes, but one strengthened by the various rumours we'd heard about the previous inhabitants of The Hovel. Mr Martin had known them personally, and it was common knowledge that about twenty years ago, when the crazy hippie still lived there, they'd had an affair. We collectively assumed this was what had ended his marriage.

"And a man who's attracted to someone like *that* must have similar habits," Lise told Rob after the old man eventually left.

"So he's a hippie, not a criminal."

"He could be both."

9

Our rekindled concern for the old man offended Monica to the core.

She became more withdrawn, leaving the house for longer periods of time, and reducing the length of her walks with the dog so as to avoid running into anyone. We took this behaviour as her confession – that she had truly been an accessory before the fact – and we were partly pleased, but we also acknowledged our failure in the offensive. We'd hoped for a confrontation, one that would open the valves and release some of the pressure. Instead, we were losing momentum, slipping slowly into the dangerous lands of a stalemate – where her Fever could brew unattended.

We didn't resent Mr Martin when he eventually escaped the safety net of our collaboration. There was a hole at the bottom of the net, and it was possible we hadn't knitted it tightly enough, but it was just as likely he had cut it himself. At some point, he'd managed to slip through the hole and gone back to his house, refusing to come out if not to drive away in his red bug without even a glance at us. He couldn't stand the idea of domesticity.

And we didn't chase after him. We couldn't. Our bodies were starting to show the first physical symptoms of weakness. They were the natural consequence of our intervention, not stopping to think we were foolishly exposing ourselves to the debilitating atmosphere of the Sister Houses and, more specifically, the leafy shedding of Mr Martin's trees.

They were the only ones still sporting their autumn colours. The leaves' prolonged existence had exacerbated their yellow pigmentation, developing in the process their own kind of deadly pollen. It was invisible to the naked eye, perhaps more so than the regular kind, but we could feel it saturating the air and obstructing our lungs.

The first one to spread the pollen was Rob. It had stuck to his clothes and hair when he crossed the street to help fix Mr Martin's red bug, and he carried it back into his house. From there the sneezes spread, the pollen flitting from one home to the other, eventually penetrating the school.

Our System, with its focus so narrowed on apprehending Monica's Fever, didn't stand a chance. It didn't even resist the assault of the leaves' infection.

We could have tried coming up with a new safety net for the old man, but as the incessant sneezes and the headaches that came with them strapped us down to our beds, we wondered instead how Monica could show no allergic reaction at all. Could her own energy give her some form of immunity to the pollinating leaves? Or was it that, having been exposed to them for some time now, she'd already discovered a remedy?

One she had no intention of sharing.

10

Lise always considered cleaning a therapeutic activity. Some gestures, simple enough not to exert the brain but done with precision, could relieve many of her pent-up frustrations.

And when she thought of meditation, she saw herself washing the dishes. A degrading task? Only if it was imposed on the washer. There was nothing more rewarding to Lise than to slip on her latex gloves, wait for the water to warm up, then soap on sponge and regular circular strokes. All resulting in a clean porcelain shimmer.

Rinsing the cutlery, Lise reached such a state of calmness she forgot about her allergies and took in a deep breath. Her health had improved, but she wasn't blooming yet, and as the cold air tickled her nose, it released a cascade of sneezes she was unable to repress. She stepped back from the sink and sighed.

The sneezes had reminded her of why she had started cleaning in the first place. Not the dirty dishes, but the house in its entirety: from the dust collecting on top of boxes in the attic to the newest photographs they'd developed (and still hadn't categorised nor stored in their respective albums). Her cleaning frenzy came from an uncommon surge of anxiety.

More than the pollinating leaves, it was our lengthy stalemate that was affecting her. Unresolved matters were Lise's greatest plague – they crawled under her skin like a vicious itching, spreading from her neck to the tip of her fingers, creating a haze in her mind. In the past few days, she had often thought of sharing this concern with the rest of us, knowing we were just as much involved, but something told Lise her confession would only spur laughter. The best she could do was drop hints to Rob, who then tried dispelling her worries, to no avail. The only way to relieve the itching completely would be to come out of our stalemate.

So she started praying at night, more than usual. Lise always preferred showing gratefulness, rather than request something she would later have to pay for. In this case, however, she was afraid her despair would lead her to act rashly, and, to avoid it, she prayed that either Mr Martin or Monica would make another wrong move, thus re-igniting the momentum.

Having placed the last clean plate into its cupboard, Lise resigned herself to an afternoon of idleness, watching a film with her allergy-infected boys, or leafing through the pages of an old magazine.

Then as she moved away from the kitchen, the door-bell rang.

She bolted to the window with unashamed excitement. The front hedges hid the face of the visitor, so Lise rushed outside, her tea towel wrapped around her hand. Lise was calm once again, residues of her meditation still lingering in her mind. She even smiled upon discovering that the visitor was none other than Monica; but then she noticed the frown on the woman's face and checked her smile, greeting her with a simple *hello*.

Emilia was standing beside her mother, looking down at her feet.

"Apologies for calling on you like this, but I need to ask for a big favour."

"Of course, anything."

Offering unconditional help was a risky business, and Lise squeezed the towel a little tighter at the *of course, anything.* Her parents had taught her that requesting the details of a favour before agreeing to help was rude and selfish. They'd also said she should disregard friendship or animosity and always offer the same quality of help. As a child, Lise had rebelled against that doctrine. Did everyone deserve such unconditionality? Wasn't asking for details proof of intelligence? With a few more years of life experience, she understood that the person asking for an unconditional favour was morally bound to reciprocate the gesture, at any given time. The risk that lay behind that *of course, anything* was then socially insured. Regardless, every time Lise allowed people to use that wildcard, she couldn't help wonder if that was the day *anything* would be her ruin.

"Can Emilia stay with you for a couple of hours? I have an emergency in the city, but I'm afraid I don't know how long I'll be —"

"No worries! She can stay for as long as you need. We'll take good care of her."

Monica bent over her daughter and kissed her on the forehead. She whispered to her what sounded like words of comfort, then thanked Lise before rushing into her shiny black car and driving away.

Emilia waited for the car to turn the corner, then she entered, cautiously, following Lise back into the hallway of the house. While they waited for Lise's daughter to join them downstairs, the girl stood there, looking around at the shoes strewn about the floor and the coats hanging from the rack.

"Would you like anything to drink? Or eat?" Lise asked in her most cheerful host voice.

"No, thank you. We've just had lunch, and I'm still digesting."

Lise chuckled, "Okay."

Finally, Emilia moved, intrigued by the sound coming from the living room. She walked very quietly and, when she stopped behind the couch, neither Rob nor the boys sensed her presence. She stared at the screen and frowned at a fight scene.

"That's unrealistic," she said.

The boys turned, surprised by the unknown voice. They couldn't think of a good comeback. Luckily, their silence was filled by the sound of their sister stomping down the stairs, then stopping, right there, on the last step.

Gabi eyed the newcomer. She had met Emilia at Al's birthday and hadn't particularly appreciated her boisterous laugh.

"Is it a sleepover?" Gabi asked.

"Oh," Lise paused. "I don't know about that yet."

Emilia skipped over to Gabi and hugged her.

"Should we go to your room?" she asked.

But Lise had another plan in mind. How would the girls like to make their own afternoon treat and bake some cookies? Gabi shrugged, but Emilia was keen. She claimed to be a very good baker.

"Is that so? Well, baking it is, then!"

Lise led the two girls into the kitchen. She was pleased by her spell of vivacity in suggesting this activity, but also intrigued by the cheeky tone of Emilia's response. It was a very Monica-esque thing to say, and why had we never considered Emilia as a crucial actor in our intricate street System? The things this girl knew, the things she was told! All those funny little anecdotes and countless tales, no doubt, of her dear mummy's audacity.

"Here's the recipe."

Gabi hesitated, but Emilia's eyes shone with excitement. She took hold of the recipe and read each line carefully, repeating the instructions aloud for the sake of her partner. Then she began ordering out instructions, showing Gabi how to sift the flour, break the eggs, and mix the ingredients together. Gabi obeyed without complaint.

Lise watched carefully as the two girls chatted away. She knew she should take advantage of this congenial atmosphere, but it wasn't easy steering Emilia in the right direction.

"So you bake often?" Lise asked the girl when Gabi turned away to fetch another spoon.

"I try."

"Is it a family ritual?"

"Just with *Mami*."

"And what do you do with your dad?"

"Well, Dad travels a lot. He doesn't live with us."

It was a full stop, but the way Emilia poured the milk into the batter, with slow consideration, told Lise there was more to come.

"We're still a family, though."

Lise nodded and chose to step back for a moment.

The girls' voices carried all the way to the living room and Rob decided to follow that pleasant sound. As he entered the room, there was no doubt to him what Lise was doing, seeing her eyes bright, her torso slightly leaning towards Emilia: he'd lived long enough with her to recognise the signs of an interrogation. And although he wasn't on board with this plan – it being bad form to ply a child for information – he did nothing to stop it.

Looking at Emilia, he noticed her cheeks were red and that she kept fanning herself with her hands. Lise had noticed this too.

"Emilia, are you warm?" Rob asked. "Why don't you take off your jumper?"

The girl mumbled, fiddling with the sleeves of her

jumper. She peeled it off slowly, trying to cover her arm, where a large rash shone, spreading from her wrist all the way up to her elbow. Lise took a step towards the girl, but Rob stopped her.

"Can you make me a coffee, please?" he asked her.

Lise sighed then turned towards the coffee maker.

Gabi eyed her parents but continued baking. It was almost as if she too had worked out her mother's plan and decided to play along. Yes, Lise liked to think that at least one of her children had inherited her spiritual wisdom.

"You don't go to my school," Gabi said, taking a spoonful of batter and dropping it onto the carefully buttered tray.

"No, I go to another one. They teach me Spanish there."

"Where?"

"At the other school, in SG."

"Where's that?"

"Up there," Emilia answered, vaguely pointing her finger behind her and slightly upwards.

Gabi turned and tried to follow the direction of the finger, but she couldn't locate this other school through the window. Later, she would ask her mother for some clarifications, but in the meantime, something else caught her eye.

"What about your neighbour?"

"Who? The old man?"

Gabi nodded.

Emilia shrugged. "He's weird."

Lise, who was pouring the freshly brewed coffee into two separate cups, put down the pot quietly, listening.

"Really, why?"

"I dunno… he goes in and out of his house with plastic bags."

"Why is that weird?"

"He could be dismembering bodies."

Gabi looked up from the batter, eyes wide. She waited to find a sign of humour on the girl's face, but there was none. Emilia had said this without the slightest hint of doubt in her voice. Not a quiver. A nervous laugh escaped Rob's lips.

The two girls kept quiet for a minute, while Gabi added one more mound of batter onto the tray. Then, she stopped and looked up again.

"Couldn't it just be groceries?"

"That's what Mami said, but she didn't seem too convinced about that."

"What does *she* think he might be doing?"

Emilia shrugged again. "I don't know. She didn't say anything. Just that lonely people sometimes do weird things."

The girl had understood that "the old man" living beside her had lost his mind to loneliness. She had seen it in many films and read it in her books. Still, at only nine years of age, the fundamental form of that observation was perhaps all she was prepared to accept. Emilia sensed there were deep roots stretching underneath that base, but it was best not to look there.

"She never denied my idea, though," Emilia added.

Raising the cup of coffee to her lips, Lise took a deep inhale. Only a wild imagination could be satisfied with this explanation. Then again… was Emilia truly the one behind that theory? Couldn't it be that the girl had been influenced by her mother's delusions? It would certainly explain Monica's rash decision in getting the police involved. And although Lise was eager to dig deeper into this, the girls were now done. They placed the tray of cookies in the oven and set a timer. Fifteen minutes.

They looked at each other.

"Do you want to wait in my room?"

Emilia nodded and the girls skipped away, taking their laughs and conversation with them, leaving Lise with a present of dirty utensils. Good, she wanted some quiet time to think.

Fifteen minutes later, the girls return with a new topic: that new TV show all the children at both their schools had started watching. They sat down at the kitchen table and gobbled down the warm cookies and milk. Perhaps Lise should have restricted the number each ate, but a bit of sugar might dissolve the image of murderers from their mind. Or it might distract Emilia from the itching on her left arm. The rash was of a soft pink hue, and now that it had been revealed, the girl didn't seem to mind about its existence. She dipped the cookie into the milk, taking a large bite as her free hand moved to the itchy elbow. The act was mechanical, which meant the rash was old.

Closer to dinner time, Lise set down an extra plate on the table for Emilia. She was hoping the girl would stay, perhaps drop one more insightful comment about her mother, but her hopes were crushed. Through the kitchen window, she saw the shiny black car reappear, and called Emilia downstairs, who rushed into her mother's arms.

"I cannot thank you enough for taking care of her," Monica said through her daughter's embrace.

"Please, it was the natural thing to do."

Monica gave her daughter the keys to their house and told her to get a head start. She then turned to face Lise.

"I hope she behaved well?"

"Oh, wonderfully! We baked."

This brought a smile to Monica's face, smoothing the frown that lingered there. Lise smiled back: the *of course, anything* had been a safe bet that day, and now she held her trump card against Monica. The thought was immensely satisfying.

They exchanged one more smile, then, as Monica took a step to leave, Lise heard herself say: "I'm sure you've noticed the rash on Emilia's arm."

Monica stopped and stood on the spot, silent. Lise regretted her words instantly, but it had felt impossible to stay quiet. She fidgeted with her hands, wondering if Monica was appraising the tone in which the information had been passed. Judging, perhaps, whether it was valuable to counterattack.

The smile on Monica's face vanished altogether.

She turned around and left.

11

It was a search for simplicity that made us reach for the autopilot in the first place.

LV was a town over a century old and we had long reached a stage in our lives where our circle of acquaintances and close relationships had stabilised, both in number and in type. If new faces joined our ranks, they came from a similar community and quickly adhered to our way of living. Feeling then no need to be socially creative, we had come up with our own automatic mode of communication: a specific set of registers, vocabulary, and topics that worked for any LV-based conversation.

There were many benefits to this language. Mainly, it allowed us to save our mental energy for our own individual activities. There was a reason many of our inhabitants had a penchant for the arts and philosophy. There were also never any turbulent discussions when the autopilot was on, which greatly pleased our System, so that soon enough the autopilot took over as our 'pre-set mode'.

But our dependence on it came with a cost.

Every once in a while, a restless instinct kicked in. We slipped away from the deadening torpor of the autopilot, awakened by a maddening hunger for words, and jumped at any occasion to speak. At the end of the day, however, we were left with the unmistakable feeling that we hadn't said enough. The sentences we managed to form on our own were pulled out of the same old bank of words; and even though we remembered there was a complexity to life beyond the circle of LV, our vocabulary was now obsolete, making it difficult to describe that distant reality or try to grasp its different nuances.

It was the reason Lise struggled to understand *why* her comment had been out of line. She wanted to explain it was merely a motherly instinct that had pushed her to question the rash – she wanted to, but couldn't say it. The dead silence of Monica's stare was so brutal that the autopilot failed, and with it crumbled Lise's entire ability to communicate. The first few weeks, she was completely voiceless, then some words managed to get through her lips, but it was months before she could produce a full sentence again.

We were all concerned for her state of being, naturally. Although we couldn't but wonder if her silence (and with it, the abandonment of any spiritual guidance) might not enable new channels of communication, might not even turn out to be the disturbance we had all been hoping for.

12

Jo still owned her old phone cord, with its red case and white rotary dialler. She rarely used it, though. There was just something about it that never quite convinced her.

The first time she saw a telephone, in the living room of her parents' house, she was intrigued by the object and proud to be one of the few families in her neighbourhood who could afford one. As the novelty wore out, however, and she became better acquainted with the rules devised for this specific type of conversation, Jo knew it wasn't the thing for her. She had always been content with the simple role of the listener: quiet in her appraisal, strategic in the comments she eventually shared.

The telephone had cheated her out of that prerogative. It had turned the silent listener into an aberration, marking her as deficient in her social skills. She was subservient to the blind person on the other side of the line, forced to produce a variety of sounds that would appease the irrational, yet common, fear that she might leave them speaking to the void. Unnecessary weight was given to each word said, turning even the most subtle inflection of the voice into a source of conflict, and Jo had no more patience for those mind games.

It was why she enjoyed the simplicity of going over to Monica's for a chat; and on one particularly cold wintry day, she decided to drop in at no. 8, to have her afternoon coffee there instead.

When she walked inside The Hovel, Emilia told her that *Mami* was on the phone but would soon be down. Jo hesitated, judging by the monotonous drone she could hear that Monica was trapped by the telephone. Yet she didn't have the heart to turn down the coffee the girl was offering her, so she followed Emilia into the kitchen, catching a glimpse of the giant cactus still looming in its spot in the middle of the living room. Perhaps the girl would stay and talk to her.

"I have two chapters left in my book," Emilia said as she brought Jo the coffee.

Jo smiled and let her go. The coffee was too hot.

She got up from her stool and moved about the room, glancing here and there at the different objects that composed it. Her pace was steady but slightly tentative, the way she'd practised often, so that an external viewer couldn't tell if she was showing impatience or curiosity. Eventually, Jo stopped before the glass door that led to the garden.

Patches of moon daisies had trickled about the lawn, starting from the left side and slowly reaching the wall separating this terrain from Anne's. What had happened to the green lusciousness Monica was so proud to display? The brush on Mr Martin's side, too, was evolving: the pollinating trees having finally shaken off most of their leaves. Jo took a hand to her nose, the skin there still raw from the endless tissues she'd gone through while her allergies were still strong.

It seemed new twigs were growing in place of the leaves. Expanding and intertwining, they created a brown cover that, once summer reached, would hide the ground under a dense shadow. But not yet. For now, the cover was still in its infancy, making it possible to see up to the front door of no. 6.

As Jo studied this view, she could hear Monica's exchange in the room above. Both tone and pace had increased exponentially. It was only then she realised the woman was speaking in her mother tongue, and Jo's first thought was that Monica was arguing with her ex-husband. But there would be no reason for them to communicate in Spanish. Or maybe they did. What was the rule in this situation? Who adopted whose language? Did they choose according to fluency, or was it mainly the alpha who decided?

These seemingly trivial questions ran inside Jo's mind in an attempt to cover the sound of Monica's voice, which had now reached a new octave. Overhearing the conversation wasn't what made the situation uncomfortable – Jo's proficiency in argumentative Spanish was non-existent anyway – it was the loud vibrations against the walls that disturbed her, and the fact they signalled a new outburst of the Fever.

Jo returned to her coffee, now temperate enough to be fully appreciated, and tried shifting her attention to the literary magazine that was lying on the counter. But when Monica's voice reached yet a higher octave, she set down both cup and magazine and stared ahead at the grey wood of the cabinets on the wall, not really listening to the voice above her but entranced by its vibrations.

The actual words held no meaning to her. What Jo could distinguish in the broken sentences and repeated vocables was the distinct sound of pleading. She recognised it from arguments in which she had starred herself. Those same rhythms and notes she once used when her husband lost his job, and with it, all motivation to do anything about it. It was the start of their gradual enmity.

Once the sound was identified, it didn't take Jo long to establish another connection: the person on the other side of the line could be none other than Monica's brother. Jo didn't know much about the man. This older sibling had only been mentioned once before, and it was to say Monica had one and that, in an act of sisterly resignation, she never claimed her part of their parents' house, leaving him to live in it. No name, but an adjective: *melodramatic*, that was the only word Monica allowed herself to use in her description of said brother. Jo had needed no more to understand the topic was off-limits.

After an extended period of silence, the sound of heels clicking on stone alerted Jo. She barely had time to consider walking out of the back door before Monica entered the kitchen.

"Sorry to have dropped in on you like this," Jo blurted out.

She was able to apologise for this careless intrusion because both women knew she had no real reason to do so. Monica's response was an extended sigh, so honest in its appraisal of the prevailing awkwardness, it managed to make Jo feel at ease at once. The sigh was accompanied by a feeble smile, and the offer of yet another coffee.

Jo accepted, with no real desire, but only for the benefit of the additional time needed for them both to compose themselves. Monica moved at once, snatching up the tin of ground coffee and looking around for a clean spoon.

That was when Jo noticed the nails: bare, and short, bitten right back to the skin.

Where had the usual almond shape and neat layer of polish gone? Monica had learnt from her father that clean hands were a sign of respect, "no matter how demeaning your job is." Hands were the main point of contact with the outside world, reaching for others' hands, grazing the air in a mixture of gestures that enriched her vocabulary… And yet, as she handed Jo her new cup of coffee, Monica withdrew her hands swiftly. She was hiding them from view, conscious and ashamed of this sign of neglect. Jo pretended not to notice, complimenting the quality of the coffee, then asking her about the latest translation she was working on.

"It's going alright. The author wasn't pleased with some of the liberties I took, but we've reached an agreement."

Was it Jo, or could the vibrations still be felt? She looked up to the ceiling. They seemed to be coming from upstairs, where the outburst had happened. Belated ripples Monica was clearly trying to cover with an endless string of words, complex details about this work-related incident she would have usually kept to herself. There were many instances in this monologue where Jo could have come to her rescue, taken control of the conversation, and allowed Monica to breathe. But her throat had closed up, and she damned the autopilot. Instead, she hoped Monica would soon have the decency to release her from the turbulent atmosphere reigning that day in The Hovel.

Even if she'd been able to talk, Jo wouldn't have known what to say. She only had a few compelling stories to tell, a few more since her separation, and she didn't want to use them as buffers, forgotten as soon as they had fulfilled their purpose. So, she nestled into the role of the phone listener, surprising even herself in the satisfaction of accurately timing her *mmhs* and *ohs* in such a way as to give the illusion she was actually listening. Only the slow movement with which Jo poured sugar into her cup, stirring the beverage, could indicate her mind was elsewhere. It remained with the vibrations above, and the complexity of the family drama they revealed.

Jo still remembered that one evening at her house, when she had innocently asked what Monica missed from her old home and a profusion of images had jumped at her: the weather, the language with its distinguishing colloquialisms and very own touch of humour, the intimacy of everyday interactions contrasting with the macrocosmic mess of politics… Monica had stopped herself, although the energy transmitted by the rapid movement of her hands suggested there was still more to uncover – that the real nostalgia lay in what was left unsaid. What life-changing factor had convinced Monica to move to LV, instead of going back home? Most likely, it was the girl's father; but there was also a strong possibility that the reason was purely materialistic.

Jo's mind was racing through all these levels of uncertainties when she realised it had been some time since she'd given any sign of awareness. Monica, however, hadn't picked up on her silence, or pretended not to. The woman's attention was elsewhere, drawn out the window; and Jo didn't need to turn around to identify its precise direction.

"I think he has a problem," Monica said.

Her eyes didn't move from the prey.

"Why do you think that?"

"He's been very fidgety lately. As if this sudden attention from our neighbours scares him."

Jo drank her coffee. That observation wasn't entirely impossible.

"Have you noticed he's been having some trouble

opening the door to his house?"

Jo set down her cup and shook her head. "I can't say I have."

"He'll make a mistake one day," Monica claimed, firm. "Just wait and see."

She turned around to see what Monica meant, but Mr Martin was already gone.

Perhaps he hadn't been there at all.

PART THREE

THE RULES OF THE GAME

When the body is weakened, a most natural tendency is to pull back. Find a comfortable nook, one preferably warm and quite small, and retreat there for a time.

A moment of respite, or why not, surrender.

Faced with this weakness, the organism, compound of matter and energy, takes over; and as the pain and vertigo are all that can be felt, the less tangible rest fades. In that very particular moment, the body lies down, stretched out or curled up, but still, so still. It reverts back to what seems like a flatter form of being, where technique and intellect cannot assist; but a form which, in fact, reminds us that if the body does survive the weakness, it is because it remains part of nature.

Sometimes all it takes to ward off the disease completely is this single moment of respite; but the line is tenuous, and the weakness might hold fast.

There is only so much the body can fight on its own.

1

What were we to do about the Annual Gathering?

We were unanimous in thinking it wiser to postpone it, and likewise aware this would be a controversial decision.

The Gathering was a staple of our community. It had been introduced by the elder Martins, around ten years to the date, when a peak in the ratings of our school had attracted newcomers to LV. We'd soon lost track of who lived around us now, and needed to find a way to gather these new faces all in one place – to know them better, and keep an eye on them. The Martins suggested a good old-fashioned potluck would do the trick, and the neighbourhood was rapidly convinced. It was repeated once, then twice, until the Gathering became a regular event.

We couldn't gather *all* of LV, of course. Neither did we want to. What mattered to us were the five streets we defined as 'our block': not a precise square, exactly, but an arbitrary area the council had delineated with a felt pen. At first, it was enough for us to be able to associate a family with their respective coordinates within the block. Then, with each passing year we managed to remember more than their names and faces; we noted down occupations, and even some leisure activities, too. It was impossible to become anything more than acquaintances with the majority of them, but the potluck sustained that ideal and kept the block pleased with LV.

As such, the Gathering came to mark a specific time of the year: easing us out of spring into the sweet release of summer, and thus developing greater significance to the block as a whole. It was a ritual the hard-working neighbours of our block had claimed as their own.

The technicalities of the event were the responsibility of *our* street, for it was *our* school that held the very first Gathering and continued to host it since. This meant it was our primordial duty to send out invitations, reminding the block to save the date. It also fell on us to decide which household would bring something sweet and which was left with the mains.

This year, however, with the first flowers of spring sprouting from their buds, the question of postponement soon began to taunt us. If it was held, we knew the focus of the Gathering would be on Monica. The other inhabitants of our block – Anne's Others – had heard of Monica's existence, naturally. The Hovel and its new owner were the latest attraction, and the parents of our school had wasted no time in sharing each development in our series. The Others had already laid eyes on her, but now they would want to be introduced.

How could we do so, what with Lise and her silence, and our complete inability to find a proper definition as to what Monica was to us?

Another problem – one perhaps just as big – was that Monica didn't know of the existence of the Gathering. This hadn't been planned. On her arrival, many of us actually thought this year's event could be made special because of the revamping of The Hovel. We would use its renovation as a message of progress, a reminder to the block that LV could always be the home for new projects – ones in line with our town's energy, of course.

Monica would have been the guest of honour.

But the absurdity of this idea had quickly dawned on us; and that same fall, overwhelmed by the first of Monica's outbursts after the power cut, we had delayed all matters of decision, pretending there was no ritual to speak of.

Definitely not, the Gathering could not happen this year.

It wasn't a decision we took lightly. We knew it would severely damage our credibility, but going through with it would surely be the final nail in our coffin.

Then came the matter of breaking the news. If we aimed for concision, our arguments would make no sense at all. If we sunk into the depths of the tale, the Others would see it as fanciful and insulting. Explaining anything seemed out of the question, so we opted for silence instead, hoping the Others would appreciate a gap year and see this as a chance to collect fresher anecdotes for the next Gathering.

2

St P's church stood two stately blocks away from us.

Its presence was felt ubiquitously. Not exactly imposed; not officially, unless one took into consideration its brown steeple towering above all other buildings and somehow always visible from wherever one stood. It was also recognisable by its temperamental bells, which tolled only at those hours which 'mattered': the climax of an argument, the summer solstice, the birth of another stray kitten... What defined an hour's significance varied from one individual to the other, with patterns that were renewed each year.

For our street, there were three specific times which marked the day and moulded all other activities around it – the three peak moments of the school: the eight o'clock bell, which sounded as the first students arrived; the eleventh hour, signalling the approaching lunch; and finally, the release of the four o'clock bell. Three moments of significant commotion – not only for the school but for our entire street, which burst alive with a crowd of parents, nannies, and even some curious onlookers.

Of those three rush-hours, only one had the added quality of causing a significant rise in anxiety. At the eleventh hour, a hundred pairs of child-size legs began to fidget in their seats, reminded by the bells of their growing appetite. But they wouldn't be freed just yet – and it was during the following half-hour that said anxiety peaked for all those around the children, the fully-grown legs.

In a matter of seconds – minutes for those ready to take the risk – these fully-grown legs had to decide if they would finish their current task or escape immediately. Delaying movement would throw them in a grey zone of uncertainty, where one small obstacle might mean colliding with the wall of nervous adults coming to feed their children. Worse still, it could mean reaching the bakery at the corner and realising that their favourite sandwich was sold out.

The conundrum of the eleventh hour expanded well beyond those directly involved with the school. The bakery at the corner, for instance, had to adapt its management of goods and time accordingly, paying careful attention to the successive waves of customers which entered with the first toll of the bell. As for the cars and trucks having to pass through our street to reach the road to SG, they had learnt to avoid this sensitive moment in time, or only approach in cases of extreme necessity; for although our street was a two-way lane, its design allowed for only one vehicle to pass at a time.

All in their own subtle way did what they could to make sure their movements around the eleventh hour wouldn't cause obstruction. Nonetheless, the possibility of a complication, some unexpected hitch that might unravel chaos, was always latent. It had occurred to us to come up with a new rule: either banning large vehicles from our road, or returning to the original one-way-only system. Yet we usually shrugged our shoulders, with a simple *it is what it is, c'est la vie*, which didn't mean we were fine with the situation, or that we never complained, but that in some way, we were fascinated by the unspoken coordination we had managed to achieve so far.

We couldn't imagine how easily this coordination could crumble.

3

Five minutes before the eleventh hour, Fran lay back in her chair and looked around her office. She felt a vigorous sense of calm, supported by the regular tempo of fingers typing on keyboards and papers being filed. Satisfied, she closed her eyes just for a few seconds, and imagined her next vacation: somewhere in the South, with sunshine, sea waves, and a different – perhaps less maddening – crowd. Fran even allowed herself the luxury of a deep and long inhale, which she withheld, saving it for whatever might come next. Soon, however, she had to let the breath go; and as she did, the rhythmic silence in the room was disrupted by the ringtone of her colleague's phone.

The woman, who was looking gravely at the planner before her, didn't react immediately. It was the unsettling stares at her purse from the people in the room that made her look up from the colourful grid and realise that, in fact, her purse was ringing. Trying to hide her surprise, she mouthed a general apology and answered.

Fran had two minutes to spare in her self-appointed break, so she lent an ear towards the conversation but was unable to make out anything significant. Her colleague was uttering only syllables, scattered and insufficiently structured to form a whole sentence. Nevertheless, these same syllables raised suspicion, and everyone inside the office stopped what they were doing to watch as the woman's expression slipped from surprise to confusion. In an agitated blur, she jumped from her chair and left the room. "My car" was all they could make out.

Fran stood up calmly and moved to the window. The office was at the front of the school, on the third floor; and if she stood, not exactly at the centre of the window but two steps to the left, she could have a full view of the street. Fran knew her colleague usually parked her car somewhere along the road, its electric blue paint easily recognisable. Her view, however, was obstructed by a large white truck blocking the road; and just as the eleventh hour tolled, Fran saw her colleague run through the street and disappear behind said truck.

"I think her car might've been hit," Fran said to no one in particular. "The road is packed with cars today... not very easy to navigate."

Five past eleven. Fran should return to her desk and work on that letter she meant to write before lunch... but there was plenty of time for that in the afternoon. Besides, the eleventh hour was so close that the focus in the room had already dispersed.

There were various speculations over what might have happened to the blue car, and Fran's colleagues asked her to describe what she could see.

"Where did she park?" one of them said.

"Does it matter?" another added.

In turning around to answer, Fran realised the importance of that detail.

The white truck was standing exactly between the Sisters, and Fran instantly made two connections. The first one was that, although the issue could have involved any of the houses on both sides of the street, it so happened it was the time of the month when cars could only park with the even numbers – the Sisters it was. The second element Fran remembered was that, only a few days earlier, we had seen Monica painting a white line on the road to delineate the exit of her garage. Technically, Monica didn't have the authorisation from the council to paint that line, but she claimed the measure was "necessary" since people – and with this she meant those connected to the school, whether staff or parents – were ignoring the Do Not Park sign on her garage, thus trapping her car inside.

A quarter past. The first parents started to arrive, standing outside the front gate of the school. They were those that lived near it, most of them Others, a few who came from farther away yet still refused to let their children eat whatever the school offered. On the other side of the white truck, the sound of loud horns reverberated, but the truck stayed put. What would happen, Fran thought, if neither the truck nor the blue car moved before the school bell liberated the children for lunch?

"Well, time for us to get moving."

Fran waved a hand at her colleagues, eyes still glued to the white truck. A line of cars was extending behind it, reaching all the way to the far-right end of the street. From afar, she noticed one parent car innocently arriving from the opposite direction.

Half-past eleven. The school bell rang. Chairs and tables were pushed back and forth, screeching against the tile floor in the classrooms. A few of the children were already in the hallway, looking for their name tag on the coat racks. Fran packed her things into her purse and rushed down the stairs to the main hallway, where she came across Al's classmates, branching off into two groups: those staying at the canteen, and the few lucky ones returning home for a homemade meal. Al spotted his mother and smiled, but Fran didn't respond, wary of what they would encounter outside.

The white truck was now barricaded within two long lines of cars. Both sides grew longer as the minutes passed, and patience was on its final reserves. Though the truck was grounded on the spot, the two lines inched closer and closer, as if the pressure might convince the truck to free the lane. Horns blared as Fran led her son quickly inside their home, then heated up leftovers from the night before: chicken, and a generous serving of mashed potatoes.

"What's happening outside, Mum?"

"Here," Fran added another spoonful of potatoes. "Eat your lunch, I'll go and find out."

Fran opened the door to another loud chorus of horns. Each honk was responded to by several others until the origin and the echoes mixed into one extensive raucous shout. In the cars closer to her Fran recognised the two mothers whose continual demands for a more organic lunch at the canteen had severely shrunk the school budget – their children did not eat at the canteen. They saw her and simultaneously pointed forward as if asking her to explain what the commotion was all about. Fran had no better answer than a shrug and that neutral smile she had perfected over the years to tackle any sort of complaint.

Walking away from them, Fran moved in the direction of the truck; but as she reached it, she stopped right behind it, worried about what she would discover on the other side. Over the wailing of horns, however, Fran was surprised to discern a fairly calm exchange of words. There were three voices, all female: Monica's, the loudest of the three and with the subtlest of foreign accents; her colleague's, slightly more high-pitched than Monica's but less imposing; and a third voice she didn't recognise.

"I'm telling you, there's no need to worry about that," Monica was saying. "Look – it's just cream, not paint. It'll come off in a second."

The unidentified voice laughed: "That's actually really clever."

"I didn't think they would break the window to

impound it…" Monica continued. "But I hope you understand, I was frustrated: people don't respect the sign."

There was a pause before the unidentified voice said: "Alright, well ladies, I think we're ready to move the car now. Ma'am, you'll have to come and get it at the pound."

Fran considered approaching the three women – there couldn't be anything wrong in that action alone – but she hesitated, taking a step back, remembering her delicate status: yes, Fran had finally realised that, although it was beneficial to use her connection to the school when dealing with us neighbours, the reverse situation brought her more problems than anything else. Besides, she had to think of our tricky situation regarding the Gathering. She couldn't bring attention to herself.

The less she knew, the better.

And so, she left the scene and walked back to her side of the street. From there, she watched as the third voice, now identified as a policewoman, began shouting instructions through her megaphone. The horns slowed to silence. Some drivers left their car to study the situation and took it upon themselves to relay the instructions down the lines. It was tricky to come up with the right strategy, each pawn on the board being manned by someone who couldn't see beyond the range of their own car. A few cars moved to the side; others reversed. Bumps and scratches were avoided by mere centimetres and, eventually, they found the right combination of movements.

The white truck drove away, dragging the blue electric car which Fran could now see had a smashed windscreen and a large white stain on its hood.

The three women watched the whole manoeuvre, silently. The policewoman offered to drive Fran's colleague to the pound, and as they got into the car, Monica checked her watch. Half past twelve. The street was slowly emptying, but some lingering cars remained, parents who didn't know what to do now. Would they be able to drive home and return on time for the first afternoon class? A few decided to park their car and run to the bakery. Hopefully, they would find something left.

Monica stared at the white line she had drawn. Then, walking back inside The Hovel, she returned seconds later with paint and a brush. Fran watched her as she added one fresh layer of paint, and another, until the line shone white.

A quarter to one. Fran returned to the kitchen, where her son had finished his meal; had even licked the mashed potatoes from the plate, and was now watching television. She stood behind him, laid a hand on his head, and stroked his hair.

"So what was that all about?" he asked.

"Someone stepped over the line."

4

And with that first step, the flow of those following behind intensified.

The chaos that unravelled that day proved our coordination wasn't as smooth as we had imagined. But, until then, it had been enough to deal with the risk of such a traffic jam. This new outburst of the Fever – for clearly that was what we were facing – couldn't be overlooked. Would the same incident have happened if Monica hadn't been so protective of her white line?

It was clear now that the scope of her outbursts could stretch beyond the boundaries of our street; and when the tale of that day's chaos, travelling from house to house, expanding with every new mile, reached the Others, that's when they awakened.

They had a few concerns – and many, many questions. Mainly, they hadn't been fooled by our omission of this year's Gathering. They had picked up on it almost immediately. The truth was we'd been too reliable all these years for it to pass by unnoticed.

But if it turned out we had nothing to hide, then it meant we had actually forgotten about the Gathering. Neither of these two answers were deemed acceptable and so, using the incident to their advantage, they decided it was time to speak up. Why not even suggest a change in management?

They had never dared doing so before, respectful of the pre-established rules they'd met when first arriving to LV. They had trusted that the veterans knew what they were doing. But this latest outburst of the Fever was sending a very different message. It suggested that our environment wasn't so rigid and airtight as it had seemed. LV was evolving, and anyone could lay claim to this new order. The rules of the game could, after all, be changed.

In itself, this awakening wouldn't have caused immense trouble, but the Others hadn't been informed of Lise's silence; and when they sent a delegate our way, he went to speak to her directly, as had always been the case since the elder Martins had retired from the front post.

"We have a proposition," the delegate said with no previous introduction.

Lise, who had only meant to take out the rubbish, hadn't expected such an encounter. She looked beyond the stout man on her doorstep, towards the empty street, then behind her. She was trapped. It was a weekday, and her family was dispersed and occupied elsewhere: no one could come and save her.

The hour of this meeting had been premeditated,

of course. The delegate himself, a retired man of sixty-seven with as much free time on his hands as he thought Lise had, was the one to suggest it: the idea was to catch Lise whenever there would be no motherly or wifely duty she could escape to.

Despite this scheming, it should be noted the delegate came peacefully. He had no intention of causing a scene, and relied on Lise's eagerness as a spiritual guide to guarantee the amiability of the conversation. He couldn't have foreseen that this precious quality had been shaken by the misfortune of her silence.

The delegate waited for her to say something – really, anything at all. Lise stared blankly ahead. What she dreaded most wasn't revealing her "sickness" (as she had named her silence) but to be faced with the threat of impeachment and have no means to defend herself. At that moment, the more reasonable thing to do might have been to write a note, directing the delegate towards Fran, onto whom Lise had momentarily conferred her authority; but both the stress caused by her silence and this surprise rebellion made her panic, and Lise slammed the door shut.

The delegate, naturally, felt insulted. He returned to the Others with the message that our street, very simply, had "lost it." Lost our nerves, essence, whatever it was that had made us the collective force they both admired and mocked. They would later reveal to us that, after some debate, a few of them were prepared to accept our indirect appeal to postpone the Annual Gathering. That was what we were asking for, right? A bit of extra time? But the delegate managed to convince them to investigate the matter instead. If they were to foresake the Gathering, they should at least know why.

And so, they settled on a new plan of action.

5

The first few days, we didn't notice anything out of
the ordinary. It was the recurrence that alerted us to
a change in their behaviour.

The Others started detouring from their usual
paths, walking leisurely along our street when they
had no reason to be there at all. Looking here and
there. Looking for clues, perhaps. There was the hint
of a smirk on their faces, suggesting they could inter-
rogate us at any moment, but not yet – they were
enjoying the torture they were inflicting. We might
have found their unashamed voyeurism amusing, if
we hadn't understood it wouldn't end there.

Their passage, in fact, left more than a sense of
discomfort.

After a few days of their roaming, Anne noticed
that a small heap of red tiles had been erected right
in front of her house, the last one on that end of
our street. She stumbled upon it as she was taking
out the bins. She didn't know what to make of it; in
a way, it reminded her of those cairns hikers would

add to as they conquered a new mountain. Still, the discovery upset her, and she rushed back inside.

She considered sending a message to Lise but decided against it. Her sister was just starting to pronounce her first words again, and the added stress might reverse the progress.

The following days, Anne kept an eye out. She realised many of the Others were walking from the school with a red tile in their hands. When they reached her house, they placed it on top of the heap and left. More than once, she was tempted to run outside and give them a piece of her mind, but the air of absolute innocence they sported when they approached her house increased her uneasiness. If she had to leave the house, she looked away from the heap and sped away to the next street.

It was only when the heap reached a metre high that Anne decided to do her own bit of investigation. Starting from her house, she walked the entire length of our street, inspecting the pavements carefully. Sure enough, she found two of those infamous tiles just outside of Fran's house. They were identical in shape and form to the ones on the heap. The tiles could only come from the same place. Anne picked them up and made back toward her house, but she stopped midway, noticing the peculiar red and black patchwork on Mr Martin's roof: missing tiles. Quickly, she counted the number of black spots.

A confirmed match.

This didn't satisfy her. That the roof of Mr Martin's house should be shedding its red tiles was no surprise; the fact that the old man wasn't doing anything about it didn't seem out of character either. But why on earth had the Others decided to build the heap on *her* doorstep?

Walking up to her house, Anne couldn't think of anything else to do with the tiles but add them to the heap. She could have dropped them on top but sensed the gesture would in some way irritate the Others even more: the structure was less of a heap and more of a neatly designed tower, with one tile resting on the other's face so that each balanced the weight of the other in a structure that had a symbiotic quality about it. Anne crouched down and studied it, choosing where to place her two tiles so they wouldn't disrupt the structure. Then, somewhat appeased, she went back inside.

That same night, while changing to go to bed, Anne heard some movement outside her window. She peeked outside and saw a dark figure bent over the tower, though the lighting in the street was too weak to tell who it could be. The figure seemed to be packing the tiles into a bag, and something told her the figure didn't belong to any of the Others.

Anne decided it was best to look away. The less she knew, the fewer lies she would have to tell. And the next day, when we enquired about the disappearance of the tower, Anne pretended to be just as surprised.

"I slept like a log all through the night," she told us.

Lise was the only one unconvinced; but in her

condition, explaining how she could tell her sister was lying would take too long – so she, too, kept quiet.

6

She kept a vigilant watch, however, then more than ever.

In fact, it is in great part due to Lise's logbook that those months of spring are the ones we remember with most detail. The logbook had initially been a small notebook Lise used to communicate with her family. The first pages were filled with paragraphs she scribbled during dinner, still intent on guiding the conversation, while the children listened, sharing one or two sentences with each other (sometimes a subtle kick in the shin) over their plates of vegetables.

Soon, she had to accept she could no longer steer the conversation, not if she actually wanted to eat with her family. The paragraphs shortened into sentences, sometimes only words. There were even things she had learnt to mime. Her family knew her gestures, they knew how to read the creases and twitches on her face, so it didn't take them long to create a new scheme. She let go, gradually, letting her children take on the responsibility of interacting with their father, surprised at how much they understood.

She wouldn't say she was starting to enjoy her silence – Lise had spoken for so long that a few months weren't enough to adapt to this new condition – but she was learning to make the most of it. For instance, she discovered that she had thoughts that were better kept to herself: being too long to write, the effort wasn't exactly worth it. Likewise, she gained greater awareness about her intended audience, acknowledging that not everyone had the patience to read a carefully structured paragraph on the benefits of having each sibling play a different sport. In the end, Lise realised that, as for the basic day-to-day statements, they could all be said in one or two words, leaving both speaker and listener entirely more satisfied. She would hold onto these lessons once her speech returned.

The notebook, then, acquired a new use.

Previously, when Lise saw something she considered important, she would keep that information in her head, hoping her memory wouldn't fail her when the time came to tell the tale. With her silence, Lise began to note down everything she saw, even the littlest thing, deciding later what she would share with Rob.

It was then she realised just how much she saw of Monica in a day.

There was no need to actively look for her. Whenever Lise did something beside a window she would somehow catch a glimpse of Monica, moving around, rushing in and out of The Hovel. From her kitchen, Lise could see right through their living room; and if she went to the study upstairs, she could see inside Monica and Emilia's respective bedrooms. Lise really didn't look for them, they just happened to be there; and so, to compensate for her inability to speak to herself or even hum as she went through her daily chores, she wrote down her observations.

M. always takes showers before lunch.

Must have sports equipment 2ⁿᵈ floor. Comes down sweaty, with sports clothes on.

Man that came last week is back. Must be work. Sit at dining table with papers. Fake smiles.

It was also around that time Lise noticed Monica stood too many times at her window, looking out to no. 6, for it to be a coincidence anymore. This was the reason Lise read every event following the chaos of the eleventh hour from a very different perspective than ours.

7

The Others, on the other hand, had the disadvantage of entering the game midway. They couldn't have avoided misreading many of the roles of everyone involved.

Their greatest mistake was to think Monica was an intrinsic part of us.

They claimed they knew their biology – one of them was a successful surgeon – and so they believed that the real danger came when an organism turned on itself; when it didn't know how or why, and it kept searching the outside for a cause. The clock started ticking. The inner malfunction grew, travelled within, spreading, convincing other cells to rebel as well.

The chaos of the eleventh hour had made the matter very clear to them: Monica was this rebel cell. They acknowledged she wasn't an original resident, not a clone either, but perhaps she was some form of derivative. A strain cell of sorts. The Others then decided their second plan of attack would be to stir the inner malfunction, increase its potential.

In hindsight, the plan was clever.

What helped them was that Monica seemed to have chosen not to care anymore: whether it be about her interactions with us or the negative consequences her Fever had on these. We sensed this evolution, too, but couldn't wholly prove it yet. So it was that, when the second delegate approached Monica at the market, she never thought of sending him away.

The new delegate was younger and had been chosen by the Others because he had a daughter, too, Emilia's age. He had already met Monica, exchanging a few amiable words with her earlier in the year, at that same market. There was nothing in the way he moved or talked that could suggest he had practised exactly what to say. All the conditions, then, were set to make of this encounter one casual neighbourly chat.

None of us were there that day to witness the conversation. We had recently adapted our timetables so as to get to the market at the hours of lesser affluence and avoid the crowd. If we learned about this second move, it was because the grocer favoured Flo. She always bought an extra bag of everything and could easily be persuaded by the grocer's praises of a new, expensive variety of strawberries. There was also that gentle and unaffected smile of hers, which he couldn't quite resist.

The grocer didn't pick up much on the conversation – he had clients to serve, after all – but he thought it best to warn Flo: whatever had been said,

Monica had shown herself receptive to the message, nodding vigorously and shaking the young delegate's hand when they parted.

We were prepared to bet anything the Others had told her about the Annual Gathering: its existence as well as its mysterious postponement. That is what we would have done, anyway, in their position. They must have suggested she do her own bit of digging: why not play double agent? In the end, their goal was the same: overthrow our management.

Certain of our bet, we were nonetheless left wondering about the outcome.

Whatever Monica decided to do with the young delegate's message, she took her time to act on it. Meanwhile, the wheel turned and turned, never showing any sign of stopping. At times, it seemed something was making it impossible for Monica to decide if she would properly join them or not. Neighbour or Other, who would be subjected to a new outburst? Then we realised her name, too, was on the wheel. The Others had put it there.

One wrong move from her and it could mean self-sabotage.

What would happen if the wheel stopped wasn't exactly clear, however. But there was a subtle rise in the intensity of the warning signal coming from our system, and we guessed, somehow, that the reason we were trapped in the wheel was the same one that might guarantee our survival.

8

Flo had known for a while she wasn't considered a *tough* character on our street.

She wasn't the decision maker with a strong backbone, nor the handy neighbour with tools and solutions for any problem, but the one who could be consulted, always urging people to look at the "bigger picture" – which was her way of avoiding confrontation at all costs. After all those years of training in positive thinking, however, part of her believed this was a quality rather than a fault. It meant she was, perhaps, the most reasonable one.

At least she thought so, until Monica came to visit.

Flo had felt it coming, this neighbourly call. Still, she kept hoping that the more obvious choice for Monica to get information about the Gathering would be the elder Martins. Or if she were feeling sneaky, Monica could even go and see Anne, turn one sister against the other and stir trouble within the family. But despite Flo's premonition, she grimaced when opening the front door. The grimace wasn't directed at Monica herself but at what her coming implied: Flo was a loose joint she could easily work through.

That day, Monica sported the brightest of smiles, but it soon sank into a frown. It so happened Flo wasn't alone: Fran was there too. Had Flo planned it that way? Not exactly – but after the incident with the first delegate, Flo had made sure never to be quite alone in her house during the day.

She invited Monica in, hoping the message was only brief and she would remain on the doorstep; but Monica accepted and stepped forth into no. 7. If there was still any doubt about it, Flo's hesitant pace as she led Monica to the living room made it very clear who had the upper hand.

What bothered Flo, more than this unexpected irruption, was the feigned attitude Monica was presenting: with a warm smile and a soft tone of voice that made Flo feel at ease no matter how clearly she knew it was a trap. These features would keep Flo tossing and turning all night, fretting over the underlying message of Monica's visit, over this stubborn inkling: that the solution – to the Gathering, the Fever, and all the rest – was right there, and she had missed it.

Yet in that moment, as they sat down round the coffee table, Flo felt too uneasy to act upon this hunch, and she let Fran take the reins. Would Monica have phrased things differently if it had been just the two of them?

"Are you joining us for coffee?" Fran asked

through a tentative smile, handing her a freshly-filled cup, which she accepted absent-mindedly. "We —"

"One of the neighbours told me a small celebration is hosted at the start of the summer — well, *usually*," Monica interrupted. "They're surprised nothing has been communicated about it yet."

Monica paused, dropping a lump of sugar into her espresso; and as she did so, Flo wondered if "celebration" had been a term used by the young delegate, or if Monica had misinterpreted the nature of the Gathering. No one had anything to celebrate. The ritual was ceremonial, rather than an authentic expression of conviviality.

"I don't know how you usually go about organising this celebration," Monica continued. "But I would very much like to help — if I can."

This final addition raised eyebrows.

"I can't see why you couldn't," Fran replied. "After all, the Annual Gathering is precisely about coming together and strengthening the bonds of the neighbourhood."

"Great. Well in that case —"

"But unfortunately, there won't be a Gathering this year."

Flo looked down to her feet. There was a stain on the rug she hadn't noticed before. It had that horrible intermingling shade, browning along the edges, which told her it wasn't new but still fresh. Which of her twins had done it?

"Why not?" Monica asked.

Fran set down her cup on the saucer and sighed.

Flo knew that sound. It was a sigh whose precise curtness suggested to its audience they were only embarrassing themselves by pressing the matter any further.

"*Well*," Fran began, briskly. "It seems the school is undergoing some renovations right around the time of the Gathering, so it would be quite impossible to host it there."

Flo turned sharply to Fran. It was a smart excuse, but Flo also knew Fran would never lie about matters of the school. The lies could easily come out, diminishing her influence over the next PTA meetings.

Monica seemed sceptical.

"There are other places where we could host it – this Gathering."

Was that a coffee stain though? Flo should make sure of its nature before accusing the twins. She had read in a psychology magazine that wrongful blaming could have traumatic repercussions on the children. Especially if it made the twins turn on each other.

"There's the park next to the St P's church, or –"

Fran chuckled at the audacity. "It has to be a neutral ground."

"*Neutral?*" Monica frowned. "In what way, exactly? Because it seems to me that the school isn't exactly neutral either."

"What do you mean by that?"

"It's just pretty clear who holds control over it."

Fran leaned back on the cushions behind her, her

spine a straight, tense line.

"Why are you suddenly so interested in the Gathering?"

The hint of a smile coloured Monica's eyes.

"Well, I *just learned about it… and this would've been my first one. It'd be a shame to miss an opportunity to meet the other neighbours in the block, don't you think?"*

"I'm sorry, then. I guess it's just all… bad timing."

They both nodded, but Flo couldn't decide who had won the argument, so she asked: "Do any of you know how to wash a coffee stain from a rug?"

Fran ignored the question, staring ahead at the dark cloud gathering above no. 6. Monica simply shook her head.

Finally, she thanked Flo for the coffee and stood up. Flo quickly rose too, stepping to the side to let Monica pass. She looked at Fran, waiting for her to rise as well, but she didn't. Fran smiled curtly from behind her cup, then took a biscuit and bit into it, dubiously.

Monica's gentle tap on the shoulder made Flo start for the door.

Out on the front step, Monica turned around with a definite smile.

"Shame about the rug. How do you feel about a good spring cleaning?"

Flo chuckled. She had no idea what that meant.

9

Fran's loophole might have been surprising, but it wasn't a lie.

She was still holding some resentment over the incident of the eleventh hour, mostly because it had been impossible for her to remain detached, no matter how much she tried. For one, her colleague, the one with the electric blue car, had become fearful of her: flinching whenever Fran got near her, as if the mere fact that Fran lived next to Monica made her an accomplice. Fran hadn't known what to say when the woman told the team she had decided a two-hour-long commute was safer than facing another incident like that day; or when she revealed the fees she had to pay for both the mechanic and the impound lot.

Then, there were the parents at the school, who thought they could come forth and suggest improvements to our hitherto untroubled routine, new measures that would avoid a repetition of that moment of anarchy.

Having to deal with these requests, Fran was thinking it would be wiser to distract the parents with another matter: the board of the school was considering a renovation to the playground and main hall, but debates around the budget were stalling all progress.

The idea for this renovation had come from Fran herself. She was tired of seeing the children running about the same old cement walls. More greenery, that was what she was opting for. It would increase the likelihood of them getting dirty, yes, but it would also mean upgrading their standards. "So many trees!" Emilia had once said when talking about her school in SG. Our school wasn't nearly as big, but a few more trees would do the trick.

Fran was a quick thinker – she prided herself in that – so when Monica irrupted into Flo's house, Fran took her chance. It didn't matter if Monica believed her. She knew the woman would pass on the message to the Others. That was what double agents did, right? From there on, the rumour would spread, and with both parents and the block pushing for the renovations, the board would have to accept. Two birds with one stone: her plan approved, and the Others momentarily distracted, delaying their next offensive. Yes, she was a quick thinker.

But she wasn't quick enough.

Could we blame her? The loophole could have worked but for Monica being one step ahead. It is now clear she never expected us to agree to a relocation but had aimed at a sharp refusal from the start.

Monica had wanted us to say "Strictly No Gathering" so she could come up with something else.

10

There are a number of items you can own without having a clear use for them. Throwing them away isn't often the first thought that comes to mind when in need of a change. Usually, the first step is to move them: from centre stage to the wings, the wings to backstage, and so on – until they land in a drawer, somewhere, or a box in the attic.

Once out of sight, the air feels slightly lighter. The object doesn't litter the space or one's sight, but it's not wholly irretrievable either, always within reach, if ever there is a change of heart. For some, this is a systematic process, renewed every year. Some find it rather easy to let go of objects they aren't using anymore. Many, however, feel a pang of remorse when stumbling upon the hidden object, realising they had forgotten about its existence and should probably throw it away.

There was a reason why garage sales weren't common around LV. It was an inborn trait of our energy – not so much a rejection of frugality as of exposing ourselves by revealing what we were guarding. Those things hidden in drawers and boxes were never what we were most proud of. They were reminders of our evolution, of the notions, quirks and mistakes we shed along the way. We wanted to believe their removal had meant a bettering of ourselves, and putting them on display was going against that forward movement.

Which was precisely why the garage sale was ingenious.

The proposal came through a third and final delegate. A middle-aged woman in a pastel trouser suit and with bright, fizzy eyes. She was sent directly to the elder Martins, where she assured them that the Others would take care of all the logistics. Perhaps some of the money could even be collected for the school?

We couldn't refuse. If there was an escape hatch, wasting time to find it was an unnecessary risk. The wheel turned, sentencing us all, and we were left to see who would play along, who would only reveal a few things and who would be suicidal enough to refuse.

11

A steady drizzle, falling on unsuspecting soil, but gently at first.

The drops soothed those spots of earth that were starting to itch from a long, dry winter, and the soil drank. It drank for days on end as we sat in front of our televisions, seven fifty p.m. on the dot, eager for the news, skipping from one channel to the other to find which forecast would announce the return of the sun. None did. The sun looked at the drizzle from afar, sometimes touching it, testing its resistance, testing its resilience; but it couldn't push it away.

Eventually, forecasters decided to skip our area altogether. Angry viewers had called to complain and sent menacing letters: they suspected it was the forecaster's negative predictions that were influencing the continual grey weather.

Then came the day when the soil finally gave up. It had drunk too much and was unable to absorb any more; so it began to expel the excess, pushing the water back to its surface, waiting for that one footstep that would press firmly on the ground and wring the surplus away.

The streets became dangerous pathways. Mud oozed, climbing up the soles of our shoes, or spurting out onto the back of our trousers. Bushes and trees pulled their roots out of the ground, desperate for air, and pavements lost their support. The soft gravel sank under the weight of our footsteps, creating pits that collected the endless stream of rainwater. We were forced to walk on the road instead, where we advanced slowly, cautiously, shielding ourselves behind a parked car when a vehicle drove past.

In these conditions, the return home grew long and strenuous. When the front door closed behind us, enclosing us within the safe and dry air of our houses, we told ourselves we wouldn't go outside again until the nightmare stopped. That thought brought us peace throughout dinner, but then, unwilling to be defeated by the weather, we set our alarms for the next morning and prepared ourselves for a new venture.

On the third weekend of rain, the sense of inevitability finally beat us down, and no one stepped foot outside. It was officially spring and here we were, trapped inside, circling our houses like fish in an inverted bowl, looking for something or passing the time; we couldn't tell which. Then, we noticed Mr Martin was sitting outside, on his doorstep – had been sitting there, perhaps, since the genesis of the drizzle.

The intertwined ivy covering his porch seemed to

protect him from the rain but, for the sake of security, he was holding an umbrella over his head. He had nothing with him but that flimsy thing and an old bag beside him, which his free hand held tight against his left thigh. He sat there and looked straight ahead, waiting – for someone to come or for the hours to pass – we didn't dare ask.

Some days, he would stay there until the sun set; others he gave up sooner. Either way, he eventually stood up and walked towards the brush in his back garden. There, he would get into his red bug and drive away for the night. But there were a few times when he would stay in the garden, and we couldn't tell what was going on: if he had disappeared through the back door, or if he had some other place of refuge hidden under the brush. When he did drive away, we found him right outside his doorstep the next morning. He always seemed to be the first one out, the first one ready to face the drizzle.

This show of perseverance moved us, and his routine was so perfectly consistent, we began to think there was a natural motive behind it, as if the old man was testing the limits of his will, just for the sake of it – so that the more days passed, the greater we rooted for him.

Watching him had become a new source of entertainment for Flo and Lise's children. They would rush home from school, grab a piece of baguette and a chocolate bar, and post themselves in front of their respective windows. One house would call the other and they would make bets over the phone:

how many more days, what was in the bag…

Lise's oldest, Nico, felt these little games were insulting: he believed the old man was teaching them a wise lesson, turning the dreadful weather into an opportunity for self-growth. Nico even decided he himself should take part in this spiritual venture. He packed a bag with the essentials, which, unable to ask his guru for advice, were no more than a few cereal bars and a towel in case it got a little too wet out there. His mother's firm and silent grip pulled him back inside: the old man could meditate all on his own, thank you very much.

One day, the children spotted Monica. She had finally emerged from her house, equipped with proper rain boots, a coat, and a sturdy black umbrella – so well equipped, it seemed rather excessive for something as inconsequential as drizzle. Nonetheless, her attire made the old man look like an amateur.

"I bet my candy on Monica," Gabi suddenly whispered into the receiver.

"But she's not part of the game!"

"Says who?"

Monica walked around The Hovel. Leaning over her side of the fence, she appeared to be speaking to Mr Martin. The old man took a moment before realising it was him that she was addressing, and, with a start, he lifted his face from his thighs, this childlike pose he had lately adopted, to look shyly at his neighbour.

Whatever Monica said to him, Mr Martin considered seriously, and the children inched closer to the window, staring with apprehension at the two sets of lips that no longer moved. Eventually, without a word, Mr Martin stood up, and the children gasped.

He left his ivy-formed refuge to meet Monica, who now stood waiting for him on the front steps of The Hovel. Seemingly ashamed of his defeat, he swiftly walked the path towards the front entrance, only to halt just before the final step. What would his no. 6 think of this treason?

His left foot wavered, then he quickly crossed the threshold, allowing The Hovel to welcome him inside. Or was it a welcome *back*? How many times before had he visited the Sister? We shrugged the thought away, worried the image of the hippie or the old woman (whomever he had chosen in the past to be a little too acquainted with) might come back to haunt us. We focused instead on The Hovel's front door and waited. Mr Martin re-emerged only after an hour. Without pause, he went straight to his garden, into his red car, and sped off.

The next day, we woke up to a clear blue sky. It was the start of April. None of the children, however, were in the mood for celebration – none except for Gabi, who went to school with a smile and a bag of candy double the size she had the day before. Her hunch had proven accurate: Mr Martin wasn't at his doorstep, nor was he the next day, or the day after that.

Still, the children debated what to do about their bets. They had only grudgingly surrendered their candy to Gabi, claiming her last-minute change wasn't fair play. True, no rules had been set, but they felt the end of the game was inconclusive. Their predictions had never included the possibility of an external factor coming to challenge the old man's will; and so, they decided they needed to understand *exactly* what had happened before distributing the victuals.

They rang The Hovel's doorbell and explained to Monica their situation. Had she tempted the old man with the idea of a dry and warm room? Monica sent them away, stern. The children walked back to their homes, shuffling and mumbling. Only Gabi turned around to wave back at the woman who had now adopted an aura of good fortune in her eyes.

Two weeks later, on another rain-free day, Mr Martin stood on his doorstep once again. Instead of his scrawny umbrella, he was holding a set of keys, but something appeared to be stopping him from using them. Ten long minutes passed before he inserted the right key into the hole and unlocked the door.

He took a step back and stared at the wooden panel. He waited a bit longer, throwing swift glances behind him. Eventually, he stretched his arm towards the door and gave it a surprisingly firm push. The door opened, gently, with grace; and somewhat confused, Mr Martin walked inside.

12

One other person who hadn't been too daunted by the drizzle was Jo. She had maintained her new routine, which was to go on walks along the river each Saturday morning.

The river wound around the back of LV, separating it from the next land, the hill where SG stood, with its castle and royal park. On our side of the bank, a neat gravel path had been designed for people to take walks, jog, and cycle. This path being mutually shared with the adjacent towns – cousins of LV, though less influential – it was the only place where LV-ians and non-LV-ians would merge naturally, with no apprehension or prejudice. Sports clothes and the exercise rush – they made it a little more difficult to differentiate the people in the crowd.

Jo had never taken advantage of the river path before and had only recently started to appreciate those walks, the view of the grey waters, and the cover the houses on the left side of the path provided against the town buzz. The reason behind this delay – as with her many other acts of self-censorship – trickled all the way back to her ex-husband. It surprised her not to have realised this sooner, but then one morning, as she was standing in her kitchen waiting for the coffee to boil, Jo had a moment of déjà-vu.

In the memory, she had been standing just as she did then, with her burgundy robe wrapped tight around her waist. The difference was that her husband had been sitting next to her, at the kitchen table, reading the day's paper. Jo remembered having looked out of the window and seen a similar sky, clear and blue, and she thought: wouldn't it be lovely to go out and enjoy the fresh air?

When she shared this thought with her husband, however, he'd laughed.

"Don't be ridiculous. We don't go out on walks. We're not *that* couple."

Nodding, she had turned off the stove and poured herself a cup of coffee.

That was the first time Jo had seriously wondered, *then what couple are we?* What bound them together? Apart from common offspring and a promise made before a stranger too many years ago to even remember why they thought they could keep it.

Remembering that rebuff, Jo decided that if they hadn't been *that* couple, she could very well be *that* woman now. She had spent many summers at her grandparents' old house in the mountains hiking, communing with nature. Why should a little urbanity stop her? And so, she began walking. At first, half an hour, then a full one, and then even when it rained a little. She just followed the path and waited for the moment her legs begged her to turn back around. It was simple and inconsequential, and at least it felt like she was going somewhere, anywhere – the only way to find out was to keep on going.

It was returning from one of these walks that Jo saw Monica distributing flyers.

She saw her at first from afar and recognised the dark hair and commanding posture. Monica had been dropping flyers inside every mailbox on our block. Eventually, from a closer distance, Jo saw her lingering outside no. 6.

Jo knew the flyers were about the garage sale. No one had told her about Monica's new mind game – we had stopped all communication with her ever since the first days of her treason – but at night Jo could hear the whispers travelling from one house to another. She never said a word on the subject, waiting for Monica to come in person and explain her reasoning. Jo even lingered in her house on occasions where she had errands to run, just in case Monica might pop around.

It never happened.

She wasn't exactly disappointed, but neither was she too surprised. Their last conversation, on the day of the phone call, had left Jo with the impression that, if the two women could still be friendly, neither of them felt intimate enough with the other to form a solid duo. Jo was too LV-ian for Monica's taste, unable to break from rules and concepts, and fully trust her gut instead; but Jo didn't see why she should reject that identity completely. She had enjoyed the aura of singularity Monica's proximity shed on her, but ultimately, she knew she would be safer within LV alone. At least, in the long run.

The others believed Monica's bluntness signalled there was something at the root of her personality that wasn't altogether right. In Jo's opinion, the root wasn't rotten. She knew she might have helped the root grow, but if there was one thing Jo could vouch for was its sanity.

The unchecked growths, however, were the true cause for worry. To the point where she had begun to reconsider some of our arguments. Without a doubt, the garage sale was a terrible idea; but if the other neighbours thought Monica was playing a nasty trick on them, Jo knew the real target was other. It was only fair to warn us, steer us back in the right direction. The only problem was she had vowed to herself never to get tangled in our dramas again. If she was to deliver the message, she had to find some form of bypass, a means to escape the avalanche of questions that would follow. This thought undoubtedly led her to Lise.

Much like the first delegate, Jo chose that specific time of day when she knew Lise would be completely alone. She wanted to avoid both interruptions and spectators.

When the door opened, she simply blurted out the message:

"It's all a ploy. Monica just wants to see what's inside no. 6."

With those words, Jo left, satisfied with herself.

13

Why had Emilia gone through the hole?

To get the dog. At least, that was the reason she gave, the one she repeated incessantly. There was a hole in the fence. A big one. They hadn't noticed it before because the brush on Mr Martin's side had got too dense. The bushes and vines were pushing through the wires, opening up breaches here and there, reaching out their long spindly arms towards The Hovel's back garden. Neither she nor her mum ever went that far back. It was the dog's secret place, his miniature jungle.

Emilia went looking for him. She had been in her bedroom and could hear him barking from the garden; but, eventually, she lost track of the sound. And when she went outside and called for him, she saw his little muzzle smiling at her from the other side of the fence.

"How did you get there?"

The dog barked, then disappeared inside the brush.

Emilia inspected the fence, from front to back, and there was the hole, right next to the tool shed. It was a big hole too, widened by some branches that were now growing out and *up up up*. She tried calling him through the hole, gently at first, then using her serious voice, but the dog didn't obey. Emilia thought hard. Surely this hole wasn't new. The dog must have been going back and forth for days now.

So, she went through. Without really thinking about it. It just seemed to her that, if anyone happened to find her dog on the other side, a lot of people would get upset: Mr Martin, her mum and… the others too.

The reasoning there seemed plausible, coming from a nine-year-old. If anything, it actually shone positively on her, showing not only a sense of courage in adventuring herself in that dark brush, but some responsibility as well. The dog was hers, after all.

Once on the other side, however, it wasn't as easy to find him as she might have thought. The dog was small and his coat blended well with the colour of the earth and the branches. Emilia called out, again and again, but this time she whispered. She was afraid the old man would be there and catch her.

Then Emilia spotted him, sniffing around the back door of the house. She pretended to have his treats in her pocket and called him, reaching a clenched fist towards him. The dog skipped over, and she caught him. *Snatch!*

So why, then, hadn't she gone back through the

hole?

She must have thought no one could see her. Emilia didn't understand that if the dog's coat blended well with the brush, her neon blue shirt did not. Neither did she stop to think that the window she chose to peek into was on the side of the house, exposed to the street. There was a large brick placed conveniently under it, just large enough for her two feet. Emilia glanced around and, holding the dog against her, she climbed it.

That's when Flo saw her.

She was parking outside her own house and couldn't help noticing the neon blue sparkling through the brush. At first, she didn't think twice on it – a mere trick of the light – but then, the neon blue barked, and Flo looked closer at it.

"Emilia? What are you doing there?"

Two pairs of puppy eyes stared back at her.

The girl jumped down the brick and ran towards the back, her little dog bouncing up and down against her chest.

"Emilia?"

Flo squinted, but lost sight of the pair. She crossed the white line onto no. 8, cautiously, and tried looking through the fence, scanning the garden. The dog was the first one to appear, galloping happily across the lawn. He was followed by a sharp cry.

Flo ran to the doorbell and rang wildly.

Monica's head popped out of the window on the first floor.

"What's going on?"

"Emilia's hurt! In the back, hurry!"

Ultimately, the girl suffered but a minor scratch to the arm from the loose wires of the hole. It was the scare and the rush of adrenaline that spurred her sharp cry, but there were no tears.

"It doesn't really hurt, just a tingle. But *Mami*, I saw no bodies," she said, forgetting about the injury and turning her attention to the rash still shining on the opposite arm.

Again, we asked ourselves why she had gone through the hole.

The answer might have lain in the classical dichotomy: nature *versus* nurture. A curious nature might explain why the girl decided to snoop around no. 6. She had been playing right next to it for months, seeing the brush change colour and forms as the seasons evolved. Suddenly she had an opportunity to walk that mysterious land. Any child would have done the same.

But what about that comment made when Monica took Emilia into her arms?

I saw no bodies.

Only Lise knew where that comment stemmed from. She had good reason not to remark on Monica's chosen method of nurture, still suffering the consequences of her own innocent remark, but she wouldn't stop us from investigating. And whether Monica had spoken the words to Emilia, or even hinted at the idea, once within the realm of no. 6 the girl knew what her mother would have wanted her to do. What other course could her mind take, trapped as it was between the tormenting pull of both Sisters?

The question wasn't so much why the girl had done it. The paradigm had changed. The real problem now was to understand how the Fever had passed from mother to daughter. Because if the Fever was natural, a genetic condition, then the fear of us ever contracting it was delusory: we could easily contain it, creating a solid buffer between us and any new outbursts. If the Fever was nurtured, however, then our focus would have to be on the chain of infection.

There had to be a way to protect ourselves, if not to fight it.

Whichever reality proved true, we couldn't hope to achieve satisfying results on our resources alone. No, stopping the Fever would require a combined force.

14

A plain white card and black ink.

The message was succinct, in that style Lise had now perfected and honed.

It had taken her two months to fully recover from the shock of her silence and be able to say a whole sentence, a complex one too. But she didn't really want to. Lise was enjoying the mental exercise, looking for the most effective and direct way to strike her audience. This all remained theoretical but, in the process, she found that this new style could eventually take her even further in her spiritual guidance.

Coming to terms with this idea hadn't been easy, though. Not when Lise had already spent the past year doubting her methods. Monica's interference had been her first cause of worry, but when the silence struck, Lise lost all hope: it would be impossible for us other neighbours to feel her guidance now. And yet, against all predictions, her imposed muteness strengthened her resolve.

Her silence would cling to her through her lifetime, she was certain of it. There were changes she had experienced, nerve reactions that revealed the stronghold her silence laid on her. At first, Lise felt suffocated, but soon she learned to work her way around it. Sometimes she controlled it, sometimes it was the other way around. It was in the flow of energies, a movement of shadows and light that suddenly decluttered her brain, and Lise knew, she just felt it as an inevitability, that she would be able to *say* whatever she was thinking. Likewise, an excess of noise, too much humidity in the air, would block her airway and, no matter how much she wanted it, no words would come out.

The day Jo came to see her, for instance, Lise was quite capable of responding, but she decided not to.

The air that morning was chill but light, the sun was still low enough that the Sister Houses were bathed in a soothing sepia shadow. Her airway was free. Her silence was letting her be. If she didn't respond, however, it was because there was nothing more to say. Jo's message invited many questions, but none Lise couldn't figure out on her own.

"It's all a ploy. Monica just wants to see what's inside no. 6."

The message hadn't surprised her. There was a specific page in Lise's logbook dedicated to Monica's obsession. The page was filled with questions and thoughts on the matter; and as she progressed, she wrote any new observations on that topic in a bright purple felt pen.

She had come to the same conclusion as Jo: the

garage sale had been designed with one person in mind. And if we neighbours were taunted by the idea of an exposure, then that was an added bonus.

Now that her suspicions were backed up from another reliable source, Lise felt comfortable in sharing this information with the rest of us. But not only.

Despite our initial reticence, we knew that giving the Others even the slightest hint of information would curtail Monica's progress. For progress it had been. Lise couldn't say exactly how it had come to be, but in the last months, it felt as if Monica's assaults had turned greater profits – perhaps it was that early perfume of summer that was aligning her energy with that of her native land, strengthening each outburst of her Fever. In any case, we couldn't afford to defend our position on two different fronts.

Here was where the card came in.

Lise had decided to make amends for her rebuff. She didn't want the Others to hold such a terrible impression of her, so she had decided to take the first step and include them in whatever offensive came next.

Her silence, however, advised her otherwise. Airway blocked, she struggled against herself as she looked around for a blank piece of paper. Then, in a drawer of her desk, she found the invitation for Monica's housewarming: small and plain, with black ink letters. Turning it over in her hands, Lise came to a compromise with her silence. She would keep the letter anonymous, this secretiveness adding a touch of gravity to the message that would make it impossible for the Others to ignore.

She grabbed a piece of paper and began scribbling.

So it was that, early on the next morning, Lise marched up to the first delegate's house and dropped the card in his mailbox. Lise had barely changed Jo's original words, but just enough to give the letter her own spiritual touch.

15

The Others didn't respond.

After weeks of updates on the garage sale, ideas, re-organisations and expansions (perhaps even add a musical show?), they retreated. Lise had hoped for a coalition, but their hesitation was welcome nonetheless.

It was a reaction we had expected.

Ever since the first Gathering, the Others had pretended the Sisters didn't exist. The reason behind this strange behaviour was that they had identified the two houses as a dangerous Singularity: a dot in the map of our street, perhaps even in LV as a whole, that was a little too turbulent and unpredictable. Whenever they came near the Sisters, they experienced an overwhelming sense of loss. Some were even subject to bouts of vertigo. As none of us neighbours were showing signs of suffering, the Others deduced that our constant exposure had made us insensible to the vibrations emanating from the Singularity. To them, however, it was clear that the Sisters had the potential to cause great havoc if allowed to be fed; and so, they decided to keep as far away from them as possible, both in body and in mind.

Their conviction was so powerful they managed to forget that if *they* could move away from the Sisters' aura, those living on the street could not. Until then, it hadn't occurred to them that the Gathering fiasco could have been caused by the Singularity. It was Lise's message that reminded them of our delicate situation.

The Others now feared the worst.

A delicate balance had kept the Singularity stable, but with the refurbishment of The Hovel, this balance had been disturbed. The Singularity had contracted, detaching itself from one Sister and nestling within no. 6. Suddenly, it all made sense: why the neighbours had cancelled the Gathering, why they kept to themselves and stayed in their homes as much as possible. The *Singularity* was reaching its point of implosion.

But how to proceed?

They couldn't back out of the garage sale. They had bothered the mayor too many times already with their proposals. Most importantly, in accepting Monica's offer, they had become attached to the Sisters' aura. Whatever new strategy they came up with had to be aimed at preserving the stability of the Singularity.

16

On the weekend leading to Easter, the Others called on a meeting of the block.

Their three delegates had analysed the situation carefully and decided they had to halt their offensive against our management. There was nothing more that could be done, nothing safe, without them first understanding our point of view. Thus, they proposed a debate and asked our street to send whichever representative we thought could do the job best.

Fran stood up almost immediately – when it came to matters of management, she was the one with the most practice. Yet it didn't feel safe to send her unaccompanied; therefore, somewhat inexplicably, we agreed that Lise should join her. If her silence should emerge, it could be easily misinterpreted as a sign of resolve, tempering any new ideas of rebellion from the Others.

The day of the meeting, Fran and Lise turned the corner into the Others' street, their minds filled with apprehension. Both sides equally dreaded a violent clash, some point of discord that would once and for all shatter the harmony we had managed to secure through many years of Gatherings.

Until the second she sat down on her designated chair, Lise couldn't tell what the silence had in store for her that day, but her spirits were wide awake. She claims now she intuited early on the Easter meeting would turn into a new ritual: something solemn more than welcoming, that would make sure no one should forget just how close the whole block came to self-destruction.

During two long hours, the Others fought to defend the garage sale, while our duo tried explaining why it was imperative that the block as a whole study Monica's Fever more closely before taking any further steps. The Fever, in fact, was the true source of threat – not the Sisters or their Singularity. But the Others never believed in the Fever. They were stuck on the physics of the situation, claiming that whatever happened on a biological level was the reverberation of a greater phenomenon. They were convinced Monica's reactions, the outbursts of her Fever, were caused by the Singularity alone – the woman lived *in* it, after all.

The two theories still collide within the Easter ritual and, depending on who is chosen to make the speech, the terms *Fever* and *Singularity* are carelessly interchanged. Those who were present at the meeting know the difference between these two terms – they understand the impossibility of both theories existing together – but they turn a blind eye, in honour of the meeting.

In the end, we agreed to have the garage sale, if only to appease Monica and buy ourselves some time. The Others still had to compromise and they allowed us to host the event on our street, convinced by our final argument: with the Sisters surrounded, we had better chances of controlling any possible factor of disruption. We had no doubt Mr Martin wouldn't take part in the sale, but by posting ourselves on his doorstep, we would make sure he stayed inside no. 6. With him out of sight, the energies would be contained – there could be no implosion, no possible chain reaction.

As for our own investigation into the Fever, we figured that if in those conditions Monica, for any reason, suffered a new outburst, it would confirm that the Fever was hers alone. Her inherent nature.

The entire block cooperating, that is the heart of the Easter meeting ritual.

Although we never do mention in our speeches that, between *Fever* and *Singularity*, only one of those theories proved right.

17

Perhaps it was the continuous chatter and the sparks of laughter that made the garage sale so enticing. Maybe it was the smell of grilled sausages on the other side of the street, the sizzling and the tempting smoke billowing towards the sky; children running between tables, stopping if they passed a toy that caught their eye. Or even Lise's older boy, Nico, shouting his prices, offering great deals.

Monica was seated farther away, beside the Others, where the food area had been placed. As we had suspected, she had nothing to sell, having cleaned her drawers before her move to LV. Still, we had to make sure she would be outside and, reluctantly, Lise made use of her trump card from the previous winter, her *of course, anything* offer. She asked if Monica could take care of the sweets table, bake cakes and other treats, as she had once suggested she could do. Monica accepted immediately.

The day was warm, one of those shimmering blue skies of May that throw one into the illusion of summer. The morning had passed uneventfully, and we were counting the money made on that first stretch, cheering inwardly for our thriftiness. Mr Martin had, unsurprisingly, stayed within no. 6, and as it reached noon, we began to lower our guard.

That was, of course, when he decided to make his appearance.

He had put on a nice white shirt and a pair of leather moccasins. Walking slowly out of no. 6, he made sure his gate was firmly locked behind him then stepped onto the road, merging with the flow of neighbours and other LV-ians that had travelled especially for the occasion. He was unmistakable amongst the crowd.

Those of our street closer to the Sisters immediately noticed him, but we were careful not to make any sudden moves. The Others, who were farther away, couldn't see him, but they sensed something had happened. The vibrations had changed, coming to them in frantic pulses. They saw that Monica's body had tensed as well. She sat up straight, sunglasses on to look better in the direction of the Sisters, where the sun was beating down bright.

Mr Martin walked calmly, hands in his pockets. He moved from one table to the other, smiling at us, patting children on the head. He chatted a little with Rob before continuing down the road. Fran guessed immediately where he was heading, and, in a moment of desperation, she jumped up from her chair, knocking down the table in front of her, creating a terrible ruckus. Mr Martin stopped, turned back, and helped her clean up.

"That was very clumsy of me," Fran chuckled.

Mr Martin smiled and shook his head.

"Are you on the hunt for something special?" Fran continued, unsure what to do if he actually answered. "A gift maybe?"

Mr Martin returned the book he was holding to Fran's table then placed his hands back into his pockets. She thought the move was strange, as if he were restraining himself; but he only continued smiling, placidly, and Nico, who was also watching the scene, remembered the old man under the drizzle. He was struck by the same feeling he'd had then: Mr Martin knew *something*. Something beyond the grasp of material things.

Fran couldn't stop him from moving onwards. The pulses were now rapid, less spaced out. In the distance, Monica's dog could be heard barking. Eventually, Mr Martin reached her table.

Emilia was standing next to her mother. She greeted the old man with a loud hello.

"Hello dear, how's your arm?"

So he knew. We had all been wondering. Had he been inside the house, had he seen the whole scene unfold? Why hadn't he said anything?

Monica looked down to her lap. Emilia shrugged.

"It didn't hurt much."

"You're a strong girl. Smart. But careful with that curiosity."

He winked then turned to Monica, who was staring at her daughter. She had removed her sunglasses, and a mixture of calmness and nostalgia was reflected in her eyes. She looked back at him and stood up.

"Would you like anything? Cake, or maybe one of these pastries? They're a speciality of mine, from back home."

"And every coin goes to charity!" Emilia said proudly.

"To the school," Monica corrected.

The old man pretended to hesitate, then chose the one that was clearly special to Monica. It was a small round pastry, filled with a dark sweet jam, and he ate it in one bite, rubbing his stomach playfully for the girl's pleasure. He asked for another.

"Exquisite," he said, reaching out coins to the girl.

Then he bowed his head and walked away.

We watched apprehensively, unsure why the exchange had gone so well, or what it could mean. It seemed to us something more had to happen, or else why would the old man have come out? What was the plan?

The Others grew anxious. The pulses continued, but they had increased in strength, and still today, we debate over the chain of causality, trying to decide if these pulses were coming from no. 6 – a consequence of what was brewing there – or if it was the other way around. The reasoning repeatedly stumbles upon the same obstacle: the image of Mr Martin continuing down the street, approaching the smouldering stands of sausages and other hot plates. The smoke followed him like a trail and expanded in our direction, clouding our view.

We heard it before anything else. A deafening crash. Some later described it as a growl, others a clap of thunder. It seemed to have come from right above our heads, but when the wind turned and the smoke of burning sausages faded away, we looked up to see the sky was still the same intact blue.

Anne noticed it first. Perhaps because, ever since the tower, she had been paying close attention to the tiles, making sure that the checkers on the roof of Mr Martin's house weren't multiplying.

She was walking back from her house, a fresh jug of lemonade in her hands, when suddenly she stopped and pointed to the roof.

Lise had come forward to take the jug from her. She wanted to place it on Monica's table, alongside her sweets, and contribute to what seemed to be a successful stand. She didn't notice Anne's pointed finger and tugged at the jug, but her sister wouldn't let go. *What are you doing,* she tried to say, but her throat felt dry and swollen, so she stepped back, rubbing a hand against her neck.

Only then did she notice everyone else was also staring at no. 6. There wasn't really much to see, except the roof was gone. The outside walls stood alone, a clear-cut line at the top. No beams, no bones. The head perfectly severed.

"Where did it go?" Anne asked.

We looked up, then down to our feet, all around us, looking for the red tiles, almost expecting another of those odd, well-balanced piles to appear.

The Others left their tables and came closer. They walked slowly, tentatively, as if any movement might trigger another mysterious disappearance. They joined us in the crowd we had now formed in front of no. 6, a black mass that watched and waited, afraid to blink.

"Where is he?"

The question came from the back of the crowd, echoing a thought that wouldn't come out, shocked as we were by the sight.

"Mr Martin, has anyone seen him?"

We turned around, neighbours and Others alike, to face Monica. She was standing one step away from us, her girl next to her.

Lise tried to answer but couldn't. She hadn't been paying attention to the old man, too distracted by the sales happening at her table. Besides, it was clear now that her silence was back in control. She told herself that, if her throat was swollen, it was only because of the dust that had erupted from the house and now hung in the air, falling down on them. She knew perfectly well it wasn't so.

Instead, she focused on Emilia. The girl was scratching her arm again.

"I think he left," Fran said.

"Yes," added the first delegate. He had emerged from the crowd, pair of tongs in hand and plastic apron shining. "I last saw him passing my grill. He was heading that way."

That way, as evidenced by the direction of the tongs, was the roundabout leading to either the train

station or the road to SG.

"I think he left," Fran repeated, this time with a little indignation, and she looked at Monica, expecting a reaction that wouldn't come.

"But what happened to the roof?" Flo asked.

She, too, looked to Monica for an answer – she was bound to have some information we didn't – but Monica simply shrugged and headed back to her table. As she walked away, Flo thought she heard her muttering, words that sounded like *giving up*. It made little sense. It might have only been a strained sigh.

Hoping to keep up with the good work of that morning, we copied Monica and returned each to our own tables, but the bright spirit of the day had evaporated. The burgers on the grill were now charred, and the smell of burnt meat permeated the street. Whoever wasn't in charge of their own table or food stand dispersed and eventually left. After a long hour of dead sales, we stored all the unsold items back inside our boxes and carried tables and chairs into our homes.

Only one table remained on the street.

Emilia had taken the few pastries left back to no. 8, but Monica sat there, arms folded against her chest. She was staring at the old man's house, just staring. So still she seemed petrified. When the girl left The Hovel to walk the dog, waving at her mother as they passed her, Monica vaguely smiled.

A strong wind eventually turned the tide. It shook the trees and bushes of Mr Martin's brush, but it also dove inside the hole left by the severed head and lifted a heavy cloud of dust, which floated down over Monica. Finally, she stood up.

18

The house was left with its insides exposed to the skies for over a month, and the old man was nowhere to be found.

In that time, the one who showed most concern was Fran. The school year was entering its final month and she tried avoiding ending the term on this bitter note at all costs. The gap in the landscape caused by the missing roof was too disturbing to ignore. Didn't we notice the stares? LV-ians and parents from the block looking around them warily, very few amused by the idea of another house crumbling down before their eyes. The school couldn't afford to lose them.

She tried figuring out a way of contacting Mr Martin, asking if any of us happened to have his mobile number. We didn't. Did the old man even own a mobile phone? So, she contacted the town council, then drove to the building herself when no one answered her calls. For inspiration, she even asked Lise to pull out the letter Monica had written to the council at the time of the power cut. Lise had kept a copy of it inside one of her binders should we ever need proof of how Monica had acted back then.

When the council answered, they claimed the only number they had was the house's landline. Frustrated, Fran considered contacting Monica for help: had she said or done anything else back then besides sending that letter? Quickly, however, she checked herself. She would never have acted that way before and, afraid the Fever might have finally got to her, Fran left the matter be.

With a little bit of luck, the old man still held enough affection towards the house not to abandon it completely.

19

Weeks of sunshine and little rain followed the garage sale.

We had started making up lists of items to pack for our different summer destinations: where to get the cheap packs of socks for the children to take to camp, where to buy the most precise and up-to-date travel guide. But when a team of five workers was eventually sent to no. 6, these well-oiled preparations were immediately interrupted.

Early in the morning, the five workers walked through the gate and circled the house, studying the walls and windows. They examined the crack that had recently formed on the right-hand wall, starting from an angle of the severed neck and falling diagonally to the feet of the house. We could catch glimpses of them through the brush, gesturing and debating. Finally, they turned to the front door.

They had the key for it, but it wasn't of much use, the door having been left unlocked. Still, they struggled to open it, trying each at a time then together, pushing and kicking. When the door did open, they hesitated before going in.

They started by setting up a tarpaulin over the exposed ceiling, which relieved Fran instantly. Then, they pulled from their truck a heavy array of gardening tools and started working on the front yard, chopping fledgling trees, uprooting bushes and felling trees. As they progressed, a cloud of pollen travelled across the street. It awoke old bouts of allergy, but their effect on us had lessened, and we let each sneeze come happily – our System was doing its work.

When they left on that first day, they made sure to lock the front gate but kept the door slightly ajar with the help of a brick they found on the ground. Flo recalled that it was the same one Emilia had used to look into the windows.

Next came an open container. The same five workers returned and, all through the day, they pulled out piles and piles of clutter from inside the house: boxes filled with cables, a collection of broken toasters, stacks of old newspapers, glass bottles, several radios, and bags full of red roof tiles.

The men were friendly. They were more than happy to chat with us during their breaks, coming out onto the street for a cigarette and gladly accepting our cups of coffee, our snacks. They knew – we did little to hide it – that we hoped they would tell us what no. 6 looked like inside.

"It's a death trap," they said.

There was little space to move within it, and

the times their feet actually touched the floor were rare. They could say now there was wood underneath them, but their steps still felt padded by a soft, unidentified texture. The rooms seemed much bigger than what they could actually be, with towers of miscellaneous objects rising in every direction. There were times they followed narrow passages they thought would lead them onwards but then took them into a dead end.

As they removed layers of clutter, they also discovered the precarious state of the walls. There were many webs of cracks, sometimes big enough to glimpse at the plumbing or electrical network underneath. In those conditions, the house wouldn't have resisted much longer. It had been barely surviving as it was, holding on with whatever strain of persistence had sustained it all these years.

"It's a wonder that roof didn't crumble sooner than it did."

For the next few days, we had to walk outside with scarves tied over our mouths, having trouble breathing from the dust being lifted every time the workers moved an object or piece of furniture. When they left for the night, we thought we could hear a soft complaint issuing from the depths of the house. Maybe it was a sound of relief, a long exhale of fresh air. Maybe one of the radios thrown into the container still had some battery left, and it came alive in the dead of the night.

It was a long week, but the men managed to get to the end of it.

"What next?" we asked them.

A new team was sent. With care and efficiency, they tore down the walls, then cleared the debris. All that was left of no. 6 was the ghost of a house and chopped up leaves on the ground. It wasn't easy getting used to the void, the excess of light that was reflected over the glimmering mound of dust and dirt; and we would stop for a second when passing that mound to pay our respects.

We didn't know who sent all these men, who gave the orders. We never asked. The moment Mr Martin disappeared down the street, we understood we would never see him again. There was no purpose in knowing his whereabouts. And two years later, when we received notice of his passing, we didn't investigate either. Nor did we wonder who was left with the ownership of the fallen terrain. The timing of his departure told us we should trust the old man's instinct. He had left things in order. He had known all along when and how the System would react.

20

All the while, The Hovel stood impassive, showing no sign of pain for its maimed Sister, not even as it lay fallen by its side, dissected piece by piece.

Its owner was scarcely seen. The day of the garage sale, Monica had waited for Emilia to return from her walk with the dog, then she dragged both into a taxi and left. There was a lamp lit on the first floor. It remained so for a few months, waiting for someone to turn it off.

When the debris was cleared and there was nothing left of no. 6, not even the dust that the rain had now washed away, we assumed Monica would come back. Until then, no one had questioned her departure, thinking that perhaps she had used this strange incident as an opportunity to go on holiday for the summer. Her absence didn't feel restful, however. We remained attentive, flinching whenever we saw a car parked before the gate, stepping over the white line she had painted.

Summer passed.

When someone eventually walked through that front door, it wasn't her.

Lise recognised Monica's husband immediately. He came in a taxi, arriving early in the morning and followed by a white moving truck. She saw him walking around the living room, then moving upstairs to the bedrooms, directing the people from the moving company. He helped them pack, mostly what belonged to his daughter. When the truck left, he turned off the abandoned light and pulled down all the blinds. Then he came out of the garage, driving away in Monica's shiny black car, never to be seen again.

And we kept waiting, unable to believe she would go so silently, without a warning, no final outburst.

Untenanted, the garden at the back of The Hovel started acting up, with the grass growing and growing, higher than we had ever seen it. It stopped when a rare weed appeared, sprouting between each blade of grass and covering the entire lawn with its bright purple flowers. The weed had thick stems that wound around the terrain, reaching the walls of The Hovel and grabbing it by its feet. Under its shadow, the grass vanished altogether. It seemed nothing could get through. No cat or bird wandered the garden. Too wary of the weed's thorns, they avoided The Hovel and remained perched on the wall that separated it from Anne's house, looking down apprehensively.

At first, the purple flowers remained within The Hovel's precinct, then slowly they spread towards its

Sister. Against the darkened soil, their purple pigment shone iridescent.

It wasn't until the next spring we realised the weed had spread beyond the Sisters' territory, crawling over the wall to Anne's house and settling there, too. Mrs Martin, an expert gardener, tried everything in her books but found no way to stop the invasion. The purple flowers wouldn't yield, and if we ripped them from the ground, some seed always remained, hidden deep in the soil. Waiting for us to look away to sprout.

Some suggested burning the weed, but for the move to be effective, we would have to burn it all the way to the source, the first rebel cells on The Hovel's terrain. The town council refused. The two properties were still under the name of its two missing owners. We couldn't touch them.

So we continued with our regular tricks, ripping them, spraying them with weed-killer. We had no luck. It was perhaps our fault if the breed spread even further, one tiny seed catching on to Lise's coat and crossing to the other side of the street. From there, it travelled over to Flo's, jumping over each fence, to Jo's and Fran's, until all houses on the street hosted the weed.

That's when we stopped fighting them.

Jo was the first to admit it: the weeds had their own peculiar charm, with flowers that never withered, only changing their shade of purple with the seasons. The weed presented a unified front, which eventually felt reassuring. When other LV-ians walked the street, they showed the flowers reverence, perhaps in fear they should also be contaminated.

They never were. The weed was ours. It had grown out of us, the inherent by-product of our System's protracted fight against the Fever. And if they swallowed our beloved roses and hydrangeas in the process, we thought it a decent price to pay.

You see, no one yet has come to reclaim the Sisters, whether it be the barren terrain of no. 6 or the resolute fort of The Hovel. There, the purple weed is its most ruthless, its thick shoots growing in every direction, weaving a tight net. There, the System works strongest, rebuilding damaged tissue with every passing day.

Acknowledgements

Firstly, to the team at Blackwater Press, who trusted in this story and my writing and helped me share it with the world. More specifically, to Vivien, whose expert eye brought the necessary edits that would make this book shine.

To my early readers, my tutors at the University of Edinburgh, whose teachings and encouraging words helped me find the voice that would make this story, and any other that came after, very much my own.

To my trusted league, Amanda and Natasha, who have read these pages and words more than anyone else; who have been in the world of LV since day one and never once said they wanted out.

To my parents, who have had to put up with my "writing mode" from an early age, my *Don't talk to me, I'm writing* stare. Who gave me the opportunity and liberty to turn this into more than just a passion. Not everyone has that chance, and I am thankful to them the most.

And lastly, to the stranger that picked up this book. I hope you enjoyed it.